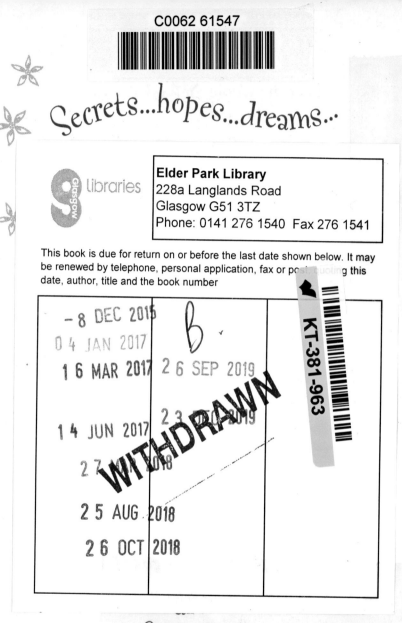

C0062 61547

Secrets...hopes...dreams...

for ever!

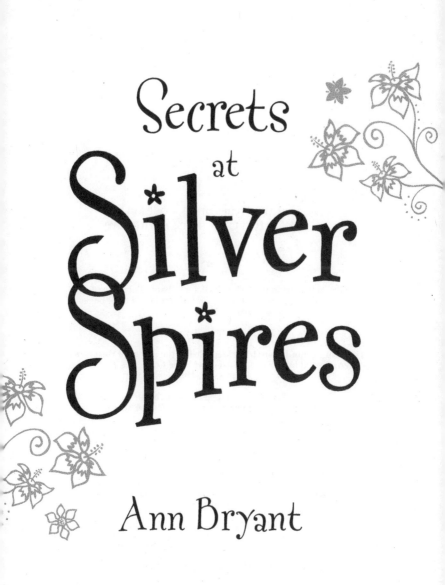

Secrets at Silver Spires

Ann Bryant

USBORNE

For the "real" Brian Hodgson
– great artist, great friend – with love

First published in the UK in 2008 by Usborne Publishing Ltd.,
Usborne House, 83-85 Saffron Hill, London EC1N 8RT, England.
www.usborne.com

Series cover design by Sally Griffin
Cover illustration by Suzanne Sales/New Division

This is a work of fiction. The characters, incidents, and dialogues are
products of the author's imagination and are not to be construed as real. Any
resemblance to actual events or persons, living or dead, is entirely coincidental.

A CIP catalogue record for this book is available from the British Library.

JFMAMJJASO D/14 01567/03
ISBN 9780746089583
Printed in Chippenham, Eastbourne, UK.

Chapter One

"That's coming on nicely, Jess."

I jumped a mile at the sound of Mr. Cary's voice because I'd been in a world of my own, blending shapes and patterns in a collage. It was my favourite lesson of the week: art. With my favourite teacher.

Mr. Cary and I both laughed at the way he'd given me such a shock.

"Sorry, Jess, I forget how absorbed you always get! I'll cough or something to warn you I'm approaching in future." He leaned forward and studied my picture carefully, then took a step back and nodded to himself. "Hmm. I like the shape that's emerging through the colours of the collage."

I frowned at my picture because I didn't get what Mr. Cary meant. I hadn't intended there to be any shape.

"Look," he said, seeing the puzzled look on my face, as his finger drew a line in the air just above the painting. "It's a shoe!"

"Oh wow! So it is!"

"Let's have a look," said my best friend, Grace, coming over from her easel. "Yes, it's a trainer!" she said, smiling to herself. "I think it's one of mine!"

I grinned at her. Some people wonder why she and I are best friends when we don't seem to have anything in common. You see, Grace is the most talented girl in Year Seven at sport and she's really good at most other subjects too, whereas I'm no good at anything except art. But Grace is a very sensitive person so she understands what it is I love about art, and when I show her stuff I've done, she doesn't just say, *Oh yes, very nice.* She asks questions and tries to see what I see. And that's lovely for me because, apart from Mr. Cary, Grace is the only person in my entire life who really understands me.

"Are you getting ideas for the art exhibition, Jess?" she asked me, her eyes all sparkly. Grace is from Thailand and when she smiles she's so pretty. Her whole face kind of crinkles and lights up.

"Just what I was about to ask, Grace!" said Mr. Cary. "I'm looking forward to seeing what you come up with for the exhibition, Jess." He smiled. "Remember, you don't have to limit your work to a painting. Or even to craftwork. Last year we had sculptures, pottery, silk screening, installation art—"

"Installation art?" said Georgie, bouncing over with a paintbrush in her hand.

"Georgie, you're dripping!" said Mr. Cary, pretending to be cross, even though everyone knows that Mr. Cary never really gets cross. None of the art teachers do. That's one of the lovely things about art – there's no need for crossness. There's no right or wrong. No horrible words. Just lovely, lovely pictures, and everyone simply slides into the magical world of whatever they're creating.

For me personally, I really feel the magic. I've always felt it, ever since I was four, moulding a ball of play dough into an elephant at playschool. I can still remember the excitement I felt as I made two thin plate shapes for the elephant's ears. I was having a little competition with myself to see if I could make the whole elephant without tearing any bits off the dough and sticking them back on again. I was trying to just keep moulding away, teasing out the legs and the trunk and the ears and the tail until the blob of dough turned into an elephant.

Then the playgroup leader said I had to stop because it was time for milk, and I remember how I cried and cried and stamped my foot until she promised to keep my elephant safe so I could carry on with it the next day. Later, when my nanny, Julie, came to collect me, the playgroup leader told her about me crying, but Julie didn't even ask to see the elephant, which made me sad.

After playschool, I got Julie to make play dough at home and I created a whole zoo. I arranged all the animals on newspaper spread right across the kitchen table, and as soon as I heard Mum's key in the front door when she got home from work – she's an accountant by the way – I rushed to the hall, grabbed her hand and pulled her through to the kitchen.

"Look!" I said proudly.

"Oooh! That's lovely, Jess!" she said, giving me a big hug. But she hadn't looked for long enough, and I think that was the first time I realized in some funny little childish way that I could see things that some people couldn't see. I mean, I'm sure the blobs of dough looked exactly that – blobs of play dough with bits sticking out – but to me there were all sorts of animals in there just waiting to be seen.

Then, when Dad got home – he's also an accountant by the way – he hardly even glanced at my zoo. He just patted my head and said, "Very nice. Let's clear it away now, Jess."

As I got older, I realized that there are two kinds of people in the world: those who kind of connect with art (that's the only way I can describe it), and those who simply don't. So that's why I feel so lucky to have Grace. I mean, the teachers at primary must have thought I was quite a good artist because they often praised me, but none of them actually wanted to *discuss* anything I'd done. Whereas Grace seems genuinely interested and says she loves trying to see the world in pictures like I do.

"I've heard that word 'installation' before," Georgie was saying. "But I don't get it. I mean an installation is like getting a washing machine or something fitted, isn't it?"

Mr. Cary chuckled, partly because Georgie had been waving her brush around while she'd been talking and had accidentally smeared green paint across her nose.

"Installation art is exactly what it says it is," said Mr. Cary. "It's all about *installing* art within its own specific environment, which might be anywhere. For example, last year," he went on, staring out of the window, "it was a piece of installation art that won first prize in the senior art exhibition. It was a birdcage hanging from a tree near Beech House, but the student had made it entirely out of natural materials and she'd left the door open to show that the bird had flown. She could have displayed the birdcage on a surface in the art room, but it wouldn't have made the same impact as it did hanging from the branch of a tree. You see, that student was making a comment about how it's not natural to keep birds in cages."

I felt my heart do the squeezing thing it does whenever I see a piece of art I love. I know I couldn't actually see the birdcage, but it was just as though I could, because there was such a clear picture of it in my head.

"That's a brilliant idea," breathed Grace. Then we exchanged a look, which meant we both understood about the birdcage.

Georgie was wrinkling her nose. "Is that *art*, though?" she said. "I mean it's very clever and all that, but…"

"Well, that's the big debate, isn't it?" said Mr. Cary. "Some people can't see it at all. Other people love it. But tell me, Georgie, if you saw an amazing piece of, say, jewellery, and it happened to be hanging from a tree, would you appreciate it?"

"Yes! Of course!" said Georgie squeakily. "You can wear jewellery. You can't wear a birdcage!"

"Jewellery?" said Katy, from the other side of me. She'd kind of jumped to attention. "You mean you can enter jewellery in the art exhibition?"

"Absolutely!" said Mr. Cary. He gave Katy a quizzical look. "I'm sure I mentioned jewellery when I told you all about the exhibition in the last lesson, didn't I?"

"No, you mentioned loads of things, but I would have definitely remembered if you'd said jewellery." Katy's eyes lit up. "That's settled. I'm definitely entering now."

"Well, that's two of you," said Mr. Cary. "Any of you others from this little group thinking about it?"

I looked round as Naomi and Mia came over to join us. We six have been friends ever since we joined Silver Spires at the beginning of Year Seven, two terms ago. We all share a dormitory called Amethyst in Hazeldean House, which is definitely the best boarding house in the whole school. Ours is actually the best dorm too, because we all get on so well together. Grace and I are best friends. Crazy Georgie is best friends with Mia, and Katy and Naomi are best friends as well.

"Well I'm not entering. No way!" said Georgie. "I can't even draw a sheep!"

Grace just shook her head. I think we all knew Grace wouldn't dream of entering. She's got so much sport going on. The summer term is even busier than the other two terms for that. Grace sometimes gets to miss prep because of tennis coaching, which is a bit worrying for me because, like I said, I'm not very good at any subject except art, and I usually count on Grace to help me when I can't spell things or don't understand something I'm supposed to have read. I know I could ask one of the others for help, but I feel a bit embarrassed about being so stupid, except with Grace because she's used to me.

Mia and Naomi both said they didn't think they'd be entering anything for the art exhibition and I wasn't really surprised. Mia has lots of extra work with her piano practice and Naomi always says she loves other people's art but doesn't think she's much good at it herself.

"Better get tidied up then," said Mr. Cary, glancing at the clock, and I felt my usual sinking feeling that the lesson had gone so quickly.

"I'll come back after lunch, Mr. Cary. Will you be here?"

He nodded. "I'm pretty much a permanent fixture in here!"

"Oh great!" said Georgie. "Can I enter *you* in the exhibition, Mr. Cary? You could be my piece of installation art!"

Lots of people heard what she said and the whole room seemed to burst out laughing. Georgie often makes that happen. She doesn't do it on purpose – she's just naturally funny. The others kept giggling all the time we were packing away, but I was quiet, because my mind was buzzing away with ideas about what I'd do for the art exhibition. Nothing was clear in my head yet. Half of me wanted to talk to Mr. Cary about it, but the other half wanted him to have a surprise. Mr. Cary's opinion means a lot to me and I know I'm not the only one who thinks he's a really good teacher. There are other girls higher up the school who've told me his students get fantastic GCSE results. In fact one of the reasons Mum and Dad chose Silver Spires school for me was because of the art department. Well, that's not strictly true. What happened was this...

At the end of Year Five, my parents asked me if I'd like to go to boarding school after primary, and at first I said yes, I'd love to, because I'd seen one of the Harry Potter films and I thought it would be really exciting and completely different from ordinary school. But then Mum casually added that if I went to a school like Silver Spires I'd probably get on better with my lessons, so then I wasn't sure about this whole boarding thing after all, in case Mum and Dad suddenly had much higher expectations of me. I liked the thought of being able to manage my work more easily though, but I knew that couldn't just happen by magic.

All through Year Six, when I wasn't painting or drawing or making things, I worked as hard as I possibly could, spending ages up in my room typing words on my computer and spellchecking them, and reading as much as I could to try and get faster at it. School was just such a struggle for me, and my biggest dread was getting left behind.

When I told Mum and Dad I didn't really want to go to boarding school, they showed me the Silver Spires school magazine with all the brilliant art in it and Mum even read out to me what it said in the school prospectus about the wonderful art department. By the time she'd finished, I wanted to go to Silver Spires more than I'd ever wanted anything in my life.

And now I'm here I'm really happy. I love boarding school. It's great having Grace and my four other good friends with me all the time, and being able to wander round such amazing grounds and go on trips and outings to art galleries and museums, and eat the most delicious food (especially puddings), and go to the art room at lunchtimes and after school and at weekends. And the classes are smaller than they were at primary, so the teacher can keep an eye on everyone all the time. Actually that's the only trouble. You see, recently I've begun to sense an awful lot of eyes on me, and I've got the horrible feeling that the teachers are beginning to realize I've got a bigger problem with reading and writing than they might have first thought.

Just as I was getting lost in all these thoughts, the bell for the end of art rang, bringing me back to the here and now.

"English next," said Naomi matter-of-factly as we left the art block.

For a second my spirits plummeted, but then like a yo-yo they swung back up again as Grace grinned at me.

"But not long till lunch, Jess. Then you can get back to your lovely art!"

I gave her a massive smile. She understands me so well. I couldn't wish for a better best friend.

Chapter Two

I looked at my name at the top of the page – *Jessica Roud* – then I looked at the big clock on the wall and sighed inside. Eight o'clock. We were halfway through prep and I'd hardly done any of my English essay. It's not that I don't know what to write. My head is bursting with ideas, but I can't get them down quickly enough because I have to look up so many words in my dictionary. Nobody else looks up half the number of words I do. I glanced at Grace, beside me. She's not in my set for English, but she was scribbling away at her own essay. She must have sensed me looking, or maybe my sigh wasn't as silent as I'd thought, because she suddenly turned to me, raising her eyebrows, and mouthed, *"Are you okay?"*

"How do you spell 'destruction'?" I mouthed back, after quickly checking that Miss Carol wasn't watching.

Miss Carol is our lovely housemistress. It's always either her or Miss Fosbrook, the assistant housemistress, on prep duty, or occasionally Miss Jennings, Hazeldean's matron. It took me a while to get used to calling homework "prep" and doing it in silence in a room with loads of other girls for a whole hour. After two terms boarding at Silver Spires, though, it feels totally normal.

Grace wrote the word down on a scrap of paper and slid it across the table towards me. The second letter was *e*. I would have put *i*. It's so much easier when Grace writes words down for me. They stand out nicely on the paper, not like the tiny little words in a dictionary, surrounded by loads of other words, impossible to find and very easy to lose. But I never ask her for easy words, because I feel ashamed about not knowing them and I don't want her to discover she's got a complete dumbo for a best friend.

"All right, girls." Miss Carol smiled. "You can finally escape this stuffy room!"

"Hurray!" went up a big cheer. Part of me loves this moment when the silence is over and I can stop concentrating, but today it was only a very small part. My essay was so short and not even finished, and I felt embarrassed about Miss Carol seeing it. So I got Grace, Mia and Georgie to pass me their prep, then I tucked my own pathetic effort in-between theirs, and handed the wodge to Miss Carol.

"Let's go outside," said Georgie. "I'm boiling hot."

The six of us decided to walk down the little lane that runs behind Hazeldean and some of the other boarding houses.

"Pity the builders have gone home," said Georgie, with a dreamy look in her eye. "That young one in charge of the cement mixer looks just like Josh from *The Fast Lane*!"

Mia laughed. "Georgie! How am I going to keep you under control?" she said, pretending to be shocked, but we're all used to Georgie with her crazy outspoken ways. Personally, I was a bit fed up with all the building work and restoration that was going on at Silver Spires. It was true that it would be wonderful when the ugly mobile rooms were replaced by lovely solid buildings that blended in with the rest of Silver Spires, but I wanted it to happen quickly so everything would be natural and beautiful and back to normal again.

"Look," I said, stopping in my tracks to stare at the streaky sunset.

"It's lovely!" said Grace, tucking her arm through mine. "I like green in the sky," she added.

Georgie grinned at me and waved her hands in front of my eyes as though she was hypnotizing me. "Are you taking it all in, Jess?" she asked in a low, slow voice, which made the others laugh.

"I expect in about fifteen minutes' time we'll see an exact copy in your sketchbook!" Mia added. "You're so clever, Jess!"

I always feel flattered when my friends say things like that, but they've no idea how wrong they are. I'm not clever at all. It's just that I can see the world so clearly through pictures, as though I'm wearing magic glasses that no one else has got.

"We'd better go back," said Grace. "Miss Carol will be locking up soon."

"It's good being allowed an extra ten minutes to go outside after prep, though, isn't it?" said Mia.

"You're joking!" squeaked Georgie. "That's like feeling grateful for one extra pea on your plate at lunchtime! Come on, let's go back to prison then!"

Mia looked shocked. "Georgie Henderson! How

can you call the best boarding house at Silver Spires a prison? Hazeldean is lovely. *And* we've got the nicest housemistress!"

"Only joking!" grinned Georgie. "I just like winding you up, Mamma Mia!"

The two of them started walking back and Grace gave me her usual look, meaning, *I'll go ahead because I can tell you're thinking about stuff.*

She was right. I watched her jogging off lightly and effortlessly and thought how much she reminded me of a gazelle. I'm very proud to have Grace as my best friend. She's the only person in Year Seven to be at Silver Spires on a sports scholarship.

Once she and the others were out of sight, I went into my own little world, wandering towards Hazeldean with my eyes on the darkening sky. I still wasn't sure exactly what I'd do or make for the art exhibition, but I knew it would be something to do with the way we all see the same things and yet we see them so differently. It was a shame I had to go inside because I wanted to keep staring up at the sky so I could capture the very second the first star came out. Maybe if I looked through the window on the stairs...

I hurried back inside Hazeldean and went up to the first floor. The window on the little landing looked out at the sunset, but didn't show enough sky for me to study the stars. It was amazing that already the sky seemed darker though. It was twenty to nine, and even though this was the beginning of the summer term, the daylight hadn't stretched itself out past our bedtime, like it would in June.

Our dorm, Amethyst, is the only one on the top floor of Hazeldean, and I love the feeling that the six of us are cosily sleeping right under the roof of this beautiful old building, with its creaky floorboards and beams and nooks and crannies. By the time I went into the dorm, the others were all getting ready for bed. I knew I should be doing the same, because it was Miss Jennings, the matron, on duty and she's very strict. It's impossible to get round her with jokes and things. Well, Georgie sometimes manages it, but not the rest of us.

As I sat on my bed with my coloured pencils and opened my sketchbook, Grace surprised me by breaking into a triumphant cheer. She's normally such a quiet person and I wondered what on earth was suddenly making her happy.

"I told you!" she said to Georgie. "But it's all right, I'll let you off the fifty pence!"

It was Katy who explained what was going on, as she came over to sit beside me. "They had a bet with

21

each other about whether you'd go straight to your sketchbook!" She laughed.

Katy loves art as much as I do, but she's more into the fashion design side of it. That's what she wants to do when she's older. She watched as I lifted the sunset from my mind and coloured it onto the paper, covering the whole page with greens and pinks and purples and an attempt at gold. I didn't like it though. I needed paints to do it justice and in the end I ripped it out, screwed it up and threw it in the bin. "It was better in my head."

"Oh no! You can't!" Grace wailed, looking as shocked as if I'd torn up a twenty pound note.

The others gasped, apart from Georgie.

"Artistic licence!" she said dramatically.

"I bet you don't even know what that is!" Katy shot at her, as she started to get into her jamas.

"Yes I do, it's…it's…" Then Naomi came back from the bathroom. "What's artistic licence, Naomi?"

Naomi frowned, then smiled. She's the wisest out of the six of us. And she's also an African princess. I love sketching Naomi because she's so graceful and upright and her eyes are big and deep. "Well, if an artist paints a picture of a bright red giraffe or something, just for the effect, that's artistic licence."

"So nothing to do with screwing up your work and chucking it in the bin?" asked Mia, with a grin at Georgie.

"I think that's called artistic temperament!" said Naomi.

"That's the one!" said Georgie.

"Yes, it sounds like what I've got!" I admitted, which made everyone laugh. Katy went over to the bin and pulled out my crumpled sunset. "Look, Naomi," she said. "It's good, isn't it?"

Naomi looked for ages, then nodded slowly. "Reminds me of Ghana. I've seen lots of sunsets like that," she said quietly, and I wondered whether she was feeling a bit homesick, because I knew she'd spent the Easter holidays in Ghana, where she comes from. She sometimes works for a water aid charity there and has told us about the awful disease and death amongst the very poor people. She says she feels guilty when she compares the lives of people in northern Ghana with her own life here in England.

After we'd all got into bed and Miss Jennings had been in to tell us to put our lights out, we talked in whispers in the dark. Sometimes we're completely quiet after lights out, but on this night my sunset seemed to have got Grace thinking.

"Isn't it amazing that it's the same sun that shines on every country in the world?" she said, sounding a bit sad.

So then I started to feel sorry for her, too, because she'd just spent the Easter holidays in Thailand and I knew she'd be missing her family right now.

"Are you thinking of painting a sunset for the art exhibition, Jess?" she went on.

"No...I don't think so..."

Georgie seemed to sigh as she turned over and I thought I ought to stop talking so she could get to sleep.

"Sorry, Georgie." I snuggled further under the duvet and wrapped myself in cosy thoughts about the art exhibition and all that Mr. Cary had told us about it in the last lesson. You're allowed to enter absolutely any type of art, but every entry has to be accompanied by a card which says a bit about it. That's the only part I'm not looking forward to, because of my terrible spelling. At least it's only a sentence or two, though, and Grace will tell me how to spell the longer words, so it shouldn't be too bad. But that still wasn't a very nice thought to take with me to sleep, so I focused on the prizes instead. There are three prizes for the junior part of the school, which is Years Seven, Eight and Nine, and three for the senior part, Years Ten and Eleven. Six prizes altogether.

And then I thought about the most exciting thing of all to do with the exhibition. Mr. Cary had told us that the famous artist, Brian Hodgson, would be coming to judge the art, and I was in seventh heaven about that. I'd seen his work at Tate Modern and I really loved it. It would be amazing if I won a prize, but nothing mattered so much as seeing Brian Hodgson, right here, at Silver Spires.

Chapter Three

The next day, during morning break, Georgie dragged us round all the places where building was going on in the school, in search of the builder she called "concrete boy". We never did find him, but I wasn't even looking. My whole attention was on the trees and the grass and the different materials being used on the building sites. My idea for the art exhibition was beginning to come into focus. I definitely wanted to create a piece of installation art and I was starting to wonder whether I might be able to use some of the leftover wood or metal from here.

At Tate Modern there are some brilliant installations. I've been there three times now – once with my parents when I was nine, once on a school trip, and once last summer with Mum and Dad and my brother, Ben, who's four years older than me and lives and breathes chess. I was the one who'd begged to go to Tate Modern and Ben had rolled his eyes and said he'd only come if we could do something that wasn't so boring afterwards. Mum and Dad had quickly agreed, because neither of them likes modern art either.

"Look at that," I remember Mum saying to Dad, in a bit of a disgusted voice, in front of one of the exhibits. She'd shaken her head in disbelief. "A room full of junk with a metal tree in the middle! What's that about?"

Dad had rolled his eyes. "How can anyone call that art?"

I'd tried to explain that the artist might have cared like mad about nature, and thought the world was being ruined with all its non-biodegradable rubbish.

"Perhaps he's put that metal tree there to make the point that as long as trees are shaped like trees, people won't notice or care if they're made of metal."

"Well if he feels that strongly about it he should write to newspapers and things, not make all this rubbish!" Ben had sneered.

And Mum and Dad had just frowned and said it was an interesting idea of mine.

"But is it really art," Dad had added, "if you have to explain it to people?"

So then I'd got into an argument with them about how art isn't anything definite, it's whatever you see in it, and that there aren't any rights and wrongs with art. And Dad said he was sorry but he thought that was airy-fairy rubbish.

I'd been furious with my family for the rest of the day, but since then I've talked all about it with Mr. Cary, and he's made me realize that there's no point in trying to get people to see what I see myself. I should just be glad that I've been born with an artist's eye.

Thinking now about that tree in the Tate Modern exhibition made me wonder whether I could create figures of people out of metal... I could feel that the idea I'd got at the back of my mind was struggling to come forwards, but it wasn't there yet, and as the others headed towards the main building, I fell behind, pictures of metal installation people filling my head. It wasn't till Grace stopped to wait for me and said, "See you after English, Jess," that I came back to earth with a horrible bump, and the light that had been glowing inside me went out.

I'm in a lower set than the others for English, maths and science. I usually like to sit about halfway back in lessons. I think that's the best place for having the least chance of being picked on to answer questions. I was in-between two girls called Isis and Lily today, but they were both talking to the people on either side of them, while I felt myself shrinking in the middle as I watched Mr. Reeves, the teacher, with a growing feeling of nervousness. He had a pile of official-looking booklets on his desk, and was slotting a piece of blank paper into each. Around me, the class chattered on.

They didn't even stop when Mr. Reeves started walking round, giving out the booklets. But then gradually the dreaded word "test" started spitting out of the chatter, like fat from a frying pan.

"Yes," said Mr. Reeves, as he returned to his desk. "Quite right. You're having a test today."

I gulped and lifted the booklet up to feel how thick it was. Then I wished I hadn't, because it was several pages and I knew that would be impossible for me to get through in one lesson.

"Now the reason for the test," went on Mr. Reeves, "is purely and simply because we want to find out about your reading levels." My heartbeat doubled. "You've got precisely thirty minutes and I think most of you will find that's quite enough…" I was sure his eyes flicked in my direction on the words "*most* of you", but maybe that was because he'd seen me looking petrified at the thought of only having thirty minutes, not even the whole lesson. "You'll find when you start reading the booklet that it's like a comprehension test, with certain things to underline in the text and other things to write down on the sheet of paper. The instructions are perfectly clear."

Yes, if you can read them. My spirits slid down to the floor.

Mr. Reeves looked at his watch, then glanced up sharply to remind us in a no-nonsense voice that we must, of course, work in silence. "Right, in a moment you will be starting the test and I shall tell you when there are ten minutes left to go, and then five minutes, and finally one." There was a dramatic pause. "You may now begin."

My heart hammered as I opened the booklet and looked at all the words and words and more words inside. Was it a story? It didn't have a title. I ran my finger very slowly under the first few words.

Read the flowing passage...

The flowing passage? Something about a stream or a river flowing along?

...then a swear the questions.

Questions. I could read that word easily as I've seen it so often, but what had that got to do with swearing or a river?

I went back to the beginning and broke down each word carefully, which was when I realized it wasn't *the flowing passage*, it was *the following passage*. Right, so I had to read the passage, then do something about swearing the questions. That couldn't be right. I made myself keep calm and sound out every letter. I still couldn't manage the one that looked like *swear*, but I kicked myself when I realized it was obviously *answer*, because of the last word being *questions*. Right, so all I had to do was read the passage and answer the questions.

Go Jess.

First I looked for capital letters so I could find out who the characters were. There was T, A and B. The B turned out to be Birmingham, which took me a while, and the T was for Tom and the A for Alex. So then I went back to the beginning and tried to decode the words one at a time, but the first sentence was so long that by the time I'd got to the end of it I couldn't remember what it said at the beginning. Perhaps it would be better to just keep reading until something made sense.

So I slowly worked out every single word on the first double page, but I still had no idea what the story was about because of having to concentrate so hard on the individual words. I think it was saying that Tom and Alex had come across a homeless person on a bench, but that might not have been it at all. Then there was a long description of clothes, but I was a bit confused about whether the clothes had been in the shop nearby or if Tom and Alex had gone to get clothes for the tramp from their home.

My mind was flooded with pictures, but then a scratching sound beside me made its way into my little world of images, and when I turned to see what it was I realized that Isis was scribbling away. She wasn't resting the sheet of paper on anything but the desk, so the ballpoint pen made quite a noise. I nearly jumped a mile when Mr. Reeves's deep voice suddenly announced that we had ten minutes to go, because I hadn't written a single word or even finished reading the passage.

I decided the best thing to do was look at the questions and get on with answering the first ones, because they were sure to be based on the first part of the passage, which I'd managed to read. Even though I wasn't at all sure what was going on in the story, I might be able to guess some of the answers. My hands were shaking as I held the booklet up a bit closer and worked my way through the first question.

Underline three words in the first paragraph that suggest that the weather in Birmingham made the atmosphere uncomfortable.

It had taken me so long to read to the end of that sentence that I'd had to go back to the beginning to remind myself whether I was supposed to underline the three words or circle them. But at least it didn't take long to find *muggy*, *dusty* and *heavy* in the passage, because I knew what I was looking for. Those words had stayed in my head as soon as I'd been able to picture the scene.

The next few questions asked you to underline more words from the text, but I wasn't so sure I'd got those ones right. And then there was a question asking us to explain how Alex's thoughts and feelings about the tramp gradually changed. Just as I understood what I had to do, Mr. Reeves announced that there were five minutes to go, so then I went into a blind panic because I hadn't written anything on the paper, and I felt so ashamed of myself.

I thought I knew how Alex felt the first time she saw the tramp because I'd pictured her walking past on the other side of the road, tutting at Tom for stopping and actually talking to the tramp. But I had no idea how her feelings gradually changed. Maybe I hadn't read that far. I spent about thirty seconds trying to find the right bit, but at the sight of Isis leaning back in her chair, looking round in a rather bored way to show she'd finished, I decided to simply make up an answer. At least the first half of it would be right.

"One minute to go," came Mr. Reeves's booming voice as I was finishing my answer. I'd written something about Alex deciding to give the tramp some clothes from her own wardrobe, only I'd stumbled over spelling *wardrobe* because it didn't look right with the two rs so close together, so in the end I crossed it out and wrote that she'd got the clothes from home.

"Right, stop working now, please." My hands were still shaking when Mr. Reeves came round to collect in the booklets and papers, and I didn't feel any calmer when we were then asked to get into groups ready for some role-play work based on the passage we'd just read.

Isis, Sophie, Lily and I formed a group together and my heart plummeted when Sophie said she wanted to play Alex because she liked the way he came to understand the tramp's situation.

He? HE? Alex was a boy not a girl. I felt like sinking through the floor with embarrassment. I hadn't even grasped the most basic thing about the passage. Thank goodness my friends didn't know anything about this test and how totally, pathetically hopeless I am.

Chapter Four

At lunch that day Georgie was the last of us six to sit down. She flopped heavily onto the bench, looking disgusted, and said, "Well I don't know about anyone else, but I've just had to suffer a ridiculous reading test. It was quite a good story actually, about a tramp, but it really annoys me when they turn it into a test!"

"We had that test too," said Mia.

I didn't like the sound of this. It seemed that the whole of Year Seven had done the same test, which meant it would definitely be talked about when the results came out and everyone would compare marks. Then my friends *would* know how totally pathetic and useless I was. I wouldn't be able to hide it any longer.

To make matters worse, as Grace got up to rush off to sports practice, she reminded me that she had tennis coaching later. "My lesson's at seven but Mrs. Mellor says it's okay for me to be late for prep."

"You lucky thing!" said Georgie. "Why don't I have tennis coaching so I get out of prep?" She frowned. "Oh yes, because I hate tennis. I knew there was some reason."

And while the others were laughing away, I sat there with a fake smile on my face, worrying about what I'd do in prep without Grace to ask for help, and worse, how embarrassing it was going to be when the results of the reading test came out.

It wasn't till I was outside on my own, looking for materials for my art installation at the building site behind the tennis courts, that I managed to forget about the reading test, and my mind became instantly flooded with more ideas for the art exhibition.

"Have you lost something?" asked one of the builders, seeing me bending down over a pile of wood shavings that I thought would make wicked hair for my installation people. My idea of what they would look like was getting stronger and stronger and I'd talked about it with Grace and the others, and they thought it was great.

"No, it's okay, I was just wondering…er…is it okay if I take a few wood shavings for something I'm doing in art?"

He grinned. "Sounds interesting. Yeah, course! All that stuff there is rubbish. It'll be swept away or burned or whatever when we've finished, so help yourself."

I nodded, suddenly happy, as I spotted some rolled-up wire netting that would make a brilliant skirt. Maybe I'd have four really different people – a man, a woman, a boy and a girl. They could be a family. A skirt made out of wire netting for the woman would be wicked. I could decorate some stiff card and put it behind the netting so it looked more like material.

The builder was back at work and the concrete mixer was churning away now, so I knew I'd have to shout to make myself heard.

"Er, excuse me, but am I allowed any of that wire netting?"

He came towards me with his hand cupped behind his ear as if to say, *Speak up!* so I repeated my question, then crossed my fingers firmly when I saw him looking doubtfully at the thick roll.

"Well, that's not exactly leftovers, you see…"

I felt instantly embarrassed. "It's okay, I was only wondering… It doesn't matter…" And I quickly gathered up my wood shavings and set off back to Hazeldean before he could say anything else.

Later, when the rest of us had met up after supper and Grace was at tennis, I showed the others the wood shavings. I'd found a black bin liner to put them in and I told my friends how I planned to keep them under my bed, along with anything else I found to add to my collection of materials. But then Katy made me think again.

"Matron will probably say you're not allowed to store those kinds of things in the dorm, Jess. Why don't you take it to the art store?"

"Yes, but people might look inside and think what a great idea Jess has got, to collect bits from the building site, and they might copy her," said Mia.

Mia was right. I'm not exactly a secretive person, but I am quite private about my art, especially when I'm creating it. I just have to be on my own to concentrate properly. Also, the art exhibition was becoming more and more important to me and it was true I felt as though I kind of owned my idea now. I wouldn't like it if anyone copied it.

"We'd better go to prep," said Naomi. "Why don't you leave it under your bed just for now?"

"Or what about that room down in the basement where our trunks and empty cases are stored?" said Katy. "I don't think anyone goes down there during term time."

So while the others went ahead to the room where we do prep, I rushed downstairs. The basement felt cold and a bit spooky, but in a funny sort of way I quite liked the atmosphere, especially when I imagined people from Victorian times living down here when Hazeldean was an ordinary house. There would have been servants living below stairs in those days. I could just picture all the wealthy important people above, having a party, while the servants rushed about cooking and cleaning and polishing glasses and setting tables.

I was deep into my daydream by the time I came to the storeroom, but I snapped straight back into the real world when I tried the handle and found the door was locked.

"Oh no!" I said crossly to the empty corridor. "Where *am* I going to keep my stuff?"

After talking to Katy and the others, I'd realized there was no way I could fit everything under my bed after all. I'd need such a lot of materials for four life-size figures. But, hang on a sec, maybe as I gradually got more stuff, the others could store some of it for me. As long as we didn't have more than, say, a bin liner full each, and as long as we pushed them as far under our beds as they'd go, surely Miss Carol and the other staff wouldn't even notice them.

I looked at my watch. I was already five minutes late for prep and I really needed that time to get through my work. I was about to rush off when I spotted a door I'd never noticed before, just along from the baggage room, and I wondered whether it might lead to a suitable storage place for my art materials. There was a plaque on the door, and other, longer words on a sign underneath. The first word seemed to be full of consonants. I stared at it for a few seconds, but there was no way I could work it out and anyway I was making myself even later for prep, so I just went ahead and tried the handle. The door wasn't locked and I stepped inside, reminding myself for a moment of the princess in *Sleeping Beauty* when she explored the palace on her fifteenth birthday and came across all sorts of rooms she'd never seen before.

This room was a real mess, with great lumps of

plaster hanging off one of the walls and lying around on the floor, and wallpaper peeling off the other walls. That would be useful. I could paste wallpaper strips and turn them into papier mâché to make the shirt for the father of my family of figures.

But then my eye roamed over the floor. Right in the middle of the room, a dust sheet was covering something large and roundish in shape and I just knew that this was going to turn out to be treasure, because from under one corner of the dust sheet something was glinting. What was it? I crept forwards and bent down so I could see it properly. And there it was – a sparkling piece of cut glass in a little teardrop shape. I gasped. It was so beautiful.

Very carefully, I drew back the dust sheet, and there before my eyes was an old chandelier, lying in pieces. Hundreds of little crystal teardrops still clung to the metal framework, some of them firmly bedded in, twinkling and glistening, some hanging by glimmering threads, and others were scattered or lying in clusters on the floor, dusty and dull. Instantly, the idea that had been hovering somewhere in my head came rushing to the front of my mind. We all see with two eyes, yet what we see is so, so different. And right now I could imagine my whole art installation, my family of four people with their angular metal bodies and glinting, teardrop eyes.

Yes!

It was impossible to concentrate on my maths prep. My maths is almost as bad as my English, but today my attention was worse than ever, wandering from the different sorts of triangles with all their varying degrees to the beautiful picture in my head of that chandelier. I slipped my hand into my pocket to feel the cold pieces of cut glass I'd gathered up in a rush just a few moments before, and felt a lovely thrill at the thought of what I'd found. What a piece of luck that Katy had suggested the baggage room as a storage place for my materials, or I'd never have come across the chandelier. But for all I knew I might have been even luckier than that. The chandelier was in so many pieces that it was probably going to be chucked out. I might have come across it just in time. I hugged my magical discovery to myself and made a decision to keep it a secret.

It was true, I'd already told Grace and the others about my metal people, but it would be so cool to keep this final finishing touch to myself. Then they'd get a big surprise when they saw the beautiful sparkling eyes set into the metal. And that got me anxious again. Where exactly was I going to create my figures? I'd got over the problem of where to store the materials, because my friends were quite happy to let me use the space under their beds, but I hadn't given a thought to actually making the artwork. I needed quite a big space, but somewhere private. Then later I could transfer the finished product to the best place for displaying it. We're allowed to place our art anywhere we want on the premises on the judging day of the exhibition, and I couldn't wait to find the perfect spot for my figures. Mr. Cary had already explained that Brian Hodgson, the judge, would be spending the whole day here on the Friday before half-term, and he'd be looking all around the school premises because the older students especially weren't limiting themselves to just hanging stuff in the art block.

I tried to pull my attention back to my maths prep but it was no good. I had to think of a place where I could work on my piece. There wasn't a single private place at Silver Spires and I felt my spirits sinking and sinking. But then something amazingly obvious popped into my head.

The secret garden. That's where I could work. Of course!

* * *

The following day after lunch I took a good look round the various places where building work was going on. It was frustrating when I kept coming across bits of scrap metal that were either too thick or too wide or too heavy, or there simply wasn't enough of any one type, because I didn't want my figures to be made of all different metals. I wanted them to look the same. That was the whole point of what my piece was about – that on the outside we're all the same (or at least our differences aren't important), but it's on the inside, where we keep our points of view and our emotions all hidden away and unseen, that we're all so different.

After school I made my way to the secret garden. It was Naomi who first discovered the garden, when she was trying to get away from the world one day. It's on the very edge of the Silver Spires boundary, way beyond the athletics field, and you just suddenly come across it behind a hedge. It's weird, because we've never seen anyone tending the plants or weeding in there and yet it usually looks cared for. It's true that the weeds grow taller and the patches of grass get longer throughout the term, but then the next term when we arrive back at school it all looks neat and tidy. We've often been tempted to ask Miss Carol about it, but the reason we don't is because we're scared that she might tell us it's strictly out of bounds and then we'd never be able to go there again.

Of the six of us, Naomi is the one who most likes to spend time on her own, then I'm next. Sometimes she and I go to the garden together, but we've got a kind of pact that we don't talk while we're there, unless we both want to.

To get to the garden you have to go quite near to Pets' Place, and that's where I saw Mia beckoning me over. She's got two guinea pigs called Porgy and Bess, and she often goes to give them a cuddle after school, or sometimes to clean out their cage. But Mia knows I'm not really into pets, so it seemed a bit weird that she was calling me over.

Even when I was a little girl I didn't want an animal that lived in a cage, because it just seemed too cruel to me. Mum once said that Ben and I could have a puppy or a kitten, but when she told us it would have to go into kennels or the cattery whenever we went on holiday, I said I didn't want one. I couldn't bear the thought of a poor little pet not understanding why it had suddenly been taken to live in a strange place with nothing and no one familiar around it.

When I got closer I could see that Mia was quite

excited about something. "Come in here, Jess!" she said, her eyes sparkling.

I followed her into the shed where the pets are kept in winter and my eyes fell on a big coil of wire in the corner.

"Hey, cool!" I breathed. "What do you suppose it's used for?"

"I think it's the stuff they make trellises with – you know, for plants to climb up walls. But is it the right thickness for your metal people?"

I grabbed a handful and twisted several strands round each other. "I could put quite a few lengths together. I might even plait it." Then I realized something and my voice fell flat. "Oh, I'm just kind of assuming I can take it, aren't I? But obviously I can't."

"All right, girls?"

We both turned at the sound of Tony's voice. I think his proper job title is Silver Spires Site Manager, but anyway, he always locks up the shed at night-times.

"Oh hi, Tony! We were just wondering what this wire is used for?"

"Surplus to requirements, I think you'd call that," he said, as he opened a large cupboard in the corner of the shed and started poking about in it.

"Surplus to requirements?" I repeated, with a careful question mark in my voice, wondering if I'd understood correctly, and crossing my fingers that I had.

"Yep, we don't need that any more. It was for making garden trellises, but we've been using the thin green stuff instead. Much more natural looking. And actually we're changing to wooden trellises now, anyway."

"So…" The little light was crouching inside me, ready to leap into a bright flame. "…could I possibly have some of it?"

"You can take the lot as far as I'm concerned. What do you want it for anyway?"

"To make something for the art exhibition."

"Nice one! Glad you can put it to good use. Don't like to see waste, myself."

"Oh thank you, Tony!"

"Any time!" He grinned, pulling something out of the cupboard, then headed off towards the rubbish dump.

I thanked Mia for spotting the wire in the first place, then rushed over to the secret garden and stood in the middle of the lawn for a few minutes, just staring into space and imagining myself working on my figures. Where could I leave them when I'd finished, though? I couldn't go lugging them back to Hazeldean, and anyway only the coiled-up wire would fit under our beds. Once I'd shaped it into the figures, they'd never fit.

Just behind the back of the garden hedge was a line of trees. I squeezed myself between the trees and the hedge and decided this would be the perfect place. I would cover my figures with bin liners and tuck them in that narrow space. They'd be safe and perfectly private there.

So everything was almost ready. I'd hidden the chandelier teardrops at the very back of one of the drawers built into my bed unit, and I'd got some bubble wrap that a teacher said I could have because it had been hanging around in a cupboard for ages. I'd decided that all my figures should look the same, with bubble wrap representing clothes. I just needed to get some more of it from somewhere or other. Georgie was begging to be allowed to pop all the bubbles, and I'd told her yes, with pleasure, because I thought it would hang better if it was flat. After that, I planned to paint it in a different colour for each figure. All I had to do now was bring my materials out here and then I could get started.

Magic.

I couldn't wait.

Chapter Five

I woke up the next day to golden sunlight streaming through the window, and felt a lovely connection to the secret garden, like a rope tugging me towards my new creation. But then a cloud passed by the window and sent a shadow sliding over my bright world. It was English first period with Mr. Reeves.

I'd managed to forget about that the previous evening when I'd been occupied with twisting and plaiting together long lengths of wire. I couldn't forget it now though. First period was just too close, and I couldn't bear the thought that we might be getting our test results.

Breakfast was a horrible anxious time for me and I could feel Grace giving me sideways glances.

"Are you okay, Jess?" she asked in the end, her forehead wrinkled in a frown.

I tried to smile brightly. "Yes, sorry. I was in a world of my own."

"I could tell… Only it seemed like a different kind of world from usual."

"No, no. Same old world!" I laughed. I didn't want Grace to know I was worrying or she'd try to get me to talk, and there was no way I could admit to anyone, not even Grace, that I was much worse than she imagined – in fact completely useless – at reading and writing. I was so ashamed of myself.

I swallowed hard and started a little chant inside my head that I kept on coming back to right up until I walked into the English room.

Please don't say anything about the test. Please don't say anything about the test…

But as I passed Mr. Reeves's desk to find a place to sit in the middle of the room, I knew my silent chanting had been pointless. The booklets lay in a pile in front of him with the papers tucked inside. I sighed and sat down heavily. Then, when we were all seated, Mr. Reeves stood up as though he was about to make a speech.

"The reading test has flagged up problems in some areas for one or two people," he said. I was glad to hear the word "two". At least I wasn't the only one, but my heart still raced away, and I knew I was going pink. I've got the kind of pale skin that goes with my auburn hair and green eyes, and I hate it when I feel embarrassed because my cheeks finish up bright red. "Sara Wynn-Jones, Frankie Pierson and Jessica Roud, you three will need to go and see Miss Cardwell in the Learning Support department. We'll start with you, Jessica, if you'd like to make your way over there...and the other two can go next time." I stood up on quavery legs, wishing I hadn't tied my hair back so it would swing in a thick curtain over my face and cover up the deep red of my cheeks as I scurried to the door. "The rest of you, turn to page fifty-four of your poetry books."

So this was it. Sara and Frankie obviously didn't have such terrible problems as me, because apparently I needed a whole session with Miss Cardwell whereas it sounded like the other two were sharing a session next time. Being in the bottom set for English, I'd always known I was one of the very worst readers in Year Seven, but, somehow, having it confirmed in front of the whole class made me feel even more of a failure. By the time I'd reached the Learning Support department, I was close to tears.

"Come in, Jessica!" came Miss Cardwell's cheerful voice. I'd never actually heard her speak before, only seen her from time to time around the school, but it didn't surprise me that her voice was so cheerful because she always wore a big friendly smile. I think she's the assistant housemistress at Willowhaven House, but it might be Oakley – I'm not sure.

"Jessica or Jess?" she asked me brightly, pulling a chair up near her own and patting the seat.

"Jess," I said in a sad little croak as I sat down.

"Jess, okay." She smiled again and looked at me carefully. "Right, nothing to worry about at all. Now that I've screened your reading test I can tell that your brain works slightly differently from other people's, but you've got lots of strengths and I must say you've coped brilliantly with your difficulties. Really brilliantly. And I want to stress right here that I am definitely not saying that you are any less intelligent than the next person. That simply isn't true.

"Now, I've just got a few questions for you, which will help me get a better idea of what your difficulties are. Tell me, do you have problems with the difference between bs and ds?"

I nodded, wondering how she knew that, but realizing immediately that it was obvious she was trained to know these things.

"And this might seem like an odd thing to be asking, but could you recite the two times table?" She broke into another of her lovely smiles and I thought what a nice, kind person she is. "It's not a trick question, Jess. Just take your time." She stopped me after six twos and I asked her if I'd done all right. "There's no right or wrong in my game, Jess," she said, looking straight at me. And I felt as though we made a little connection there, because that's how I feel about art. That's what I was trying to explain to my parents.

"Like art," I said quietly.

I didn't think she'd get what I meant, but she did, straight away.

"Exactly."

After that I had to do various other tests, like repeating sequences of numbers after she'd said them, and seeing whether I could keep my eyes following the same line of words or whether they dropped down (which they did, lots of times). And finally she said I'd done fine and I could relax.

"Well, there's obviously something going on that you need help with. What I'm going to do is talk to your parents on the phone and explain my findings, and see if they're agreeable to your having a more detailed screening by an educational psychologist. Now, you're unlikely to get an appointment before half-term, or even the summer holidays, but meanwhile we'll arrange for you to come to me, and I can help you with your reading in all sorts of ways, Jess, to make the process much, much easier for you. All right? You really should have had this kind of help at primary school, but, sadly, bright pupils like you slip through the net sometimes."

I couldn't speak. My whole mind was taken up with what people would say, and especially what my friends would say. It was embarrassing having to have extra help with reading at secondary school. I'd never live it down.

"Have you got any questions at all, Jess?"

Yes. How can you say I'm bright when I'm obviously stupid? Why doesn't my brain work properly? Why ME?

I shook my head sorrowfully, but then a more sensible question did pop into my head and I blurted it out. "Is it dyslexia? Is that what's wrong with me?"

The silence seemed to go on for ages, though it was probably only a couple of seconds really. "Yes. I think that will turn out to be the case," said Miss

Cardwell carefully. "It has to be confirmed, of course... Then you'll get the help you need – extra time in exams, someone to do the writing while you dictate what you want to say. And, Jess, you deserve these things. Dyslexia is tough, but you'll manage fine because all sorts of very clever people at the top of their professions have managed, like the artists Leonardo da Vinci and Michelangelo. So you see, you'll be in great company."

I felt like a little girl who'd gone into a sulk, because I still couldn't quite smile, even though I really wanted to when Miss Cardwell was being so kind and saying things to make me feel better. A few little pinpricks of warmth were starting to appear inside me, though, at the thought of two such famous painters sharing the same brain problems as me.

"The thing is, Jess, nature has a curious habit of balancing things out. When she creates difficulties for the brain she often compensates by handing out rare gifts..." She paused and I saw her eyes twinkle. "I have it on good authority from various members of staff here that you are a very talented artist, and I saw that you won the competition for the cover of the swimming gala programme. So there you are. That is your gift."

"It's true that I...see the world in pictures not words," I finally managed to say.

She nodded slowly, with another kindly smile. "Well, there you are. I envy you that."

Then the bell went and my horrible sinking feeling came back. How could I cope with everyone finding out I've got to have extra help with reading, like a little kid? Because, it doesn't matter what Miss Cardwell says, if you need help with reading at my age, you must be thick. The feeling seemed to drag me down so far I couldn't bear it. I didn't want people to find out, and what's more, I wasn't going to let that happen. I'd make something up. I'd pretend it was just a one-off session with Miss Cardwell because I hadn't been feeling well the day of the test so I'd done really badly. I'd say Miss Cardwell just wanted to check it was only an off-day and that there wasn't really any problem. And now she'd checked and, sure enough, everything was fine. She'd said I was perfectly good at reading and definitely didn't need any help.

Yes, that's what I'd say.

"So...when shall I come back...?" I asked hesitantly as I got up to go.

Please don't let it be during a lesson.

"Er...let me see..." She was looking in a big diary.

"Yes, why don't you come tomorrow lunchtime and Monday after school?"

"Just those two times," I said, feeling a big relief sweep through me.

"Yes, just Friday lunchtimes and Mondays after school."

"You mean I've got to come twice a week *every single week*?" It was obvious really. I didn't know why I'd ever imagined I could be turned into a normal-brained person in just two sessions.

"Yes, that's right." She was smiling away and now, once again, there was no way I could smile back. I was feeling too horrified. However was I going to be able to convince people I didn't have a problem when I had to go to the Learning Support department for reading help twice a week? And now I was going to have less time for my precious art project too. I could have cried. What a hopeless mess.

At morning break I didn't say anything to the others and I tried to act completely normally. I obviously wasn't making a very good job of it though, because Grace asked me three times if I was sure I was okay, and Mia asked me once too. In the end I said I was going to do a bit more wire plaiting and I escaped to Hazeldean and rushed up to the dorm, but I had to turn round and come back almost immediately because morning break is so short.

At lunchtime, when Grace started heading towards the table where Naomi and Katy and the other two were sitting, I panicked a bit because Isis and Sophie were also at that table. I really wanted to grab Grace and say, "Don't let's sit there today," but Katy was frantically beckoning us over, so there was no way I could say that. I followed Grace extra slowly to give myself time to think what I might say if Isis or Sophie asked how I'd got on with Miss Cardwell. And something told me they *would* ask.

"Hey, Jess," said Katy in an urgent whisper the moment I sat down. "I was wondering, how are you actually going to get your figures to stand up?"

She was leaning forwards so I leaned forward too, feeling happy that Katy was so into my art project. "I've been wondering about that too. I might have to dig them into the ground... And also, I was thinking, I must get hold of more bubble wrap—"

"Wicked! More delicious popping for me!" said Georgie loudly.

Katy and I grinned at each other, and then I started tucking into my cottage pie, but I'd hardly swallowed a mouthful when Isis's voice came over loud and clear. "Hey, Jessica, what did you have to do at Learning Support?"

I glanced up quickly and saw that both Isis and Sophie were staring at me, waiting for my answer. Then I glanced at Grace and saw a questioning look in her eyes.

Georgie was the first of my friends to speak, though. "Learning Support? Why did you have to go to Learning Support, Jess?"

"Oh that! It turned out to be a mistake." I gabbled the words at top speed because then my cheeks wouldn't have chance to turn pink. "I was feeling ill when we had that reading test, you see, so I couldn't concentrate properly. I had to go to Miss Cardwell just to check I didn't really have any reading problems. And I don't." I grabbed the jug of water and started pouring some into my glass a bit shakily, hoping like mad that I'd been convincing. I didn't dare look at Grace or the others, but I had the feeling that there were lots of pairs of eyes on me at that moment, and I knew it was really important to stay calm. "Anyone got any ideas where I can get hold of more bubble wrap?"

"I...I guess if we ask round other boarding houses?" There was suddenly something awkward hovering between Grace and me. Her eyes seemed too dark, or was it her face that seemed too pale? Or maybe I was imagining those things.

"What about asking at reception?" said Naomi. "That's where parcels and things get delivered, isn't it. They might say they can save you the bubble wrap whenever they get some."

I nodded hard, feeling relieved that Sophie and Isis seemed to have gone into their own little conversation now, and also feeling grateful to Naomi for coming up with such a brilliant idea. "I'll go along there straight after lunch. Thanks for thinking of that, Naomi."

I thought the worst had passed but I was wrong. I was just eating my apple tart when out of the corner of my eye I saw Sophie nudge Isis. Isis nudged her back and mouthed, "You," and a second later I heard my name again, and felt my skin prickling.

"We got our essays back, by the way, Jess," said Sophie. I didn't like the look on her face. It was like she was trying not to smirk. "You know, the ones we had to do in prep."

My heart started to hammer. "Oh right. Well, I'll get mine next time."

Sophie and Isis exchanged a look, which made me even more uncomfortable.

"What's going on between you two?" asked Georgie, straight out.

"Nothing!" they said, putting on over-the-top innocent looks and then grinning again.

"So what's the joke then?" asked Georgie, looking a bit indignant now.

I swallowed.

"Just something Jessica wrote in her essay," said Isis, suddenly attacking her food as though she wasn't going to say another word about it, but it was obvious she knew she'd got everyone's attention. Sure enough, Georgie couldn't resist going for the bait.

"Tell us then... What did she write?"

"How do you know what Jess wrote in her essay, anyway?" interrupted Naomi a bit snappily.

Isis glanced at Sophie. Sophie looked down. It was Isis who answered.

"Mr. Reeves put it on Jessica's desk. He thought she'd be back before the end of the lesson, you see. And he'd written something in red ink and it just kind of...stood out."

"Well, it's nothing to do with you, is it?" said Naomi, her eyes boring into Isis's.

Isis just shrugged. "Whatever."

I swallowed and looked down. Naomi had made

Isis and Sophie look very small. It was a big relief that she'd stopped them telling the whole table some spelling mistake or other that I'd made in my essay, which obviously changed the meaning of what I'd written into something really funny. But I was uneasy. I couldn't get that look on Grace's face out of my head. I didn't like deceiving my best friend.

I hated waking up on Friday. This was the day when I not only had to suffer double English, I also had to go and see Miss Cardwell at lunchtime. It was tempting to pretend I was ill and spend the day with Matron, then make a miraculous recovery in the afternoon, but I knew I couldn't do that every single Monday and Friday. I'd just have to get Grace and the others used to me going off on my own by explaining to them that I'd be using all my free time on my art project from now on.

As soon as I'd finished lunch I told the others I was going to work on my art project. "I want to give you all a nice surprise, so do you mind if I just do it on my own until it's finished? Then I'll show you."

Katy's eyes lit up. "That's a good idea. I'm going to do the same with the bracelet I'm making."

"I've got athletics," said Grace. "I'll walk with you as far as the field, Jess."

My stomach knotted. I'd be late for Miss Cardwell if I had to walk all the way to the athletics field and then come back to the Learning Support department. "Oh, I've got to go up to the dorm actually, to get some stuff."

"Oh right. See you later then. Have fun!" And with that she was gone, jogging off into the distance.

As soon as I was sure she wouldn't turn round, I rushed towards the Learning Support department, and met Miss Cardwell in the corridor, clutching a mug.

"Well done, Jess! Bang on time!" she beamed. "Right, let's get this show on the road!"

Inside her room we sat down side by side at her table, and for the next half-hour I felt completely focused because Miss Cardwell was good at helping me to understand things. I surprised myself by quite enjoying the work, and at the end I asked her if I could borrow one of the books we'd looked at. It was full of short stories and we'd started one of them but hadn't had time to look at more than the first paragraph. I was dying to know what happened next.

"I'll tell you what, I'll photocopy that page for you, Jess, because I'm going to need the book this afternoon."

As I walked back to Hazeldean to put the precious sheet away somewhere safe in the dorm, I thought about Miss Cardwell and what she'd taught me, and I couldn't help feeling happy and hopeful. It was just as though she could see right into my brain and she'd spotted a massive knotted ball of cotton and found the end. And now she was slowly starting to unravel it for me.

Chapter Six

On Saturday mornings there are lessons at Silver Spires, but once they're over, the weekend is nearly always packed with interesting and fun things to do. The houseparents are always telling us that we mustn't feel obliged to fill the whole weekend with activities, though, if we just want to chill or do our own thing or catch up on work or anything.

Sometimes there are outings or events that everyone has to join in with, like when we have international evenings and you dress up in the style of clothes from that country and eat food that is typical of the country, and maybe have dancing or singing or games, or all three. That's always great fun. Then there are shopping trips organized every week, but Grace and I don't often go on those unless we really need to buy something, because we're not that into shopping – not like Katy, who's so stylish and loves looking at all the latest fashions. It's true that I dress differently from lots of other girls at Silver Spires, but it's not so much that I'm into fashion, more that I just like putting interesting colours and styles together. And as for Grace, well she's hardly ever out of her tracksuit!

Grace often trains at the weekends actually, and I like to do my art, taking photos or drawing pictures, but if she has a match I usually go along and support her. Sometimes I have work to catch up on though, and Grace helps me. That was fine for the first term, but then during last term the work increased, and recently I haven't known where to start, there's so much. Everyone else seems to manage okay, but I feel as though I'm drowning in work because of the reading and writing taking me so long, and I can't keep asking Grace for help when she's got all her sports training to do.

Once or twice I've had to pretend I'm not interested in going to the theatre or the ice skating rink, just because I need time on my own to try and catch up with all I have to do to get through the next week of lessons. But when I had to miss a museum trip once I was so depressed and upset that I couldn't concentrate on the work anyway, so it was a waste of time.

This weekend there's an outing to the big bowlplex in town, and then the cinema later. And on Sunday there's a trip to Shakespeare's Globe. Georgie was over the moon about that and the others were going along too. I've been before with my parents, otherwise I would have loved to go, because the building is amazing. It's been built with all the materials that actually would have been used in Shakespeare's day.

The main reason I didn't want to go, though, was because I was desperate to have some time on my own to work on my project, but also to practise reading and to try and finish the story that Miss Cardwell had photocopied for me. There was one other thing that I wanted to do too. Ever since Miss Cardwell had mentioned that those two artists, Michelangelo and Leonardo da Vinci, both had dyslexia, I'd been thinking about that, wondering whether she was just saying it because she knew I was interested in art and thought it would make me feel better. After all, she could make up anything, couldn't she? And even if she genuinely thought it was true, how did anyone know for sure, when they lived so long ago?

I was determined to look them up on the internet and see what I could find out, but I knew it would take me ages and ages because I can never spell the words I want to look for. In fact I usually ask Grace to do my internet research for me. I just pretend I'm a bit useless on the internet and not sure what questions to google, and because Grace is kind and clever, she always finds me whatever I need to know. This time I was on my own though. This was private research. Embarrassing research, in fact.

I'd completely forgotten that Grace had a tennis tournament at another school on Saturday afternoon, until we met up at lunch and I saw that she had her tennis dress on.

"I'm really nervous, Jess," she told me quietly when I sat down. "This is my first proper tennis match and I've no idea how good I am compared to girls at other schools. You *are* coming, aren't you?" There must have been big doubt showing on my face because she didn't even give me time to answer. Her face was suddenly clouded with disappointment. "Or…are you working on your art piece?"

I felt terrible and didn't answer straight away because I was trying to work out if there was any way I could pack everything I had to do into Sunday, but I knew in my heart that there wasn't, because the reading would take me for ever.

"You've got all day tomorrow, remember, Jess," said Mia, tuning in. She'd only spoken in a very gentle voice and yet it still annoyed me because she had no idea what my life was like.

"Hang on! Aren't we forgetting the small matter of the Globe?" squeaked Georgie.

"I wasn't...planning on doing the Globe trip actually..." I said hesitantly.

Georgie came back immediately in a typical Georgie wrapping-up-the-conversation way. "You must be totally mad, but at least it means you can go with Grace this afternoon." Then she broke into a gabble about how great the Globe outing was sure to be. "I can't wait! The actors are the best ever, you know. I mean, when you read a Shakespeare play, you don't know what it's on about, all written in that strange old-fashioned English. But when you hear the actors speaking the words, it's like they've translated it all into modern English, because you can understand every single thing they say! And that's their skilful acting, you know!"

All the time Georgie had been making that speech I'd been wondering how on earth I was going to be able to break it to Grace that I wasn't coming with her. I knew she'd be upset, but I also knew that, being Grace, she'd try not to let it show. The others would think I was completely mad, but I'd just have to put up with that. I could simply say I'd got schoolwork to catch up on. After all, everyone knows I'm not particularly great at any subject except art. That's completely different from not being able to read properly.

I decided to speak very quietly, so no one but Grace could hear. "Would you be really, really upset if I didn't come with you to the tennis match? It's just that I so want to do my project, but also I've got quite a bit of work to catch up on." I knew I was kind of pleading with my eyes, and I hoped she understood that I hated doing this to her.

"No, that's okay. I'd probably be really nervous with you watching anyway."

There was something sort of crisp about the way Grace said that, and I noticed she didn't look at me. It wasn't like we'd had an argument, or even a disagreement, and neither of us had said anything remotely horrible. And yet the atmosphere had changed. I was confused and didn't know what to say now because I couldn't tell if Grace was cross or hurt, or just trying to make me feel better about not coming. But if that was what she was doing, then why were her eyes darting about all over the place? Or was that just because of her nervousness?

"I'd better go. I'll see you later then." She jumped up abruptly.

"Loads of luck, Grace!" I quickly said, giving her a huge smile, but she still wasn't looking, and a second later she rushed off, the others all looking a bit surprised and calling their "good lucks" after her.

"Wow, she *is* in a state!" said Georgie. "Aren't you going with her, Jess?"

"No, she says I'll make her even more nervous…"

I'd made it sound as though I'd been fully intending to go but Grace had said she'd rather I didn't, which wasn't the truth at all. And now I felt as though Naomi's all-seeing eyes were on me, and I was back to concentrating on not going red.

It was a relief when I knew the others were all safely on the coach heading for the bowlplex. I went straight to the computer room and was about to go onto the Google page when my mobile rang. I looked at the screen and saw it was Mum.

"Hello, Jessie," she said.

It was lovely to hear her voice but I couldn't help feeling a moment of panic. Had Miss Cardwell phoned Mum and explained about my learning support? That was the last thing I wanted to talk about, so before Mum had time to say another word I started gabbling away about my plans for the art exhibition. As I talked she chuckled from time to time and said she could tell I was really excited about it and it sounded wonderful. She didn't ask if she'd get to see my work and I wouldn't have known the answer to that question even if she had asked, but I got that old feeling that I've always had where my love of art is concerned – that Mum and Dad are pleased that it means so much to me, but apart from that they're not really all that interested. It's not like my brother's chess, for example. They really love the way he keeps winning matches, but, more than that, they actually want to go along and watch the matches because they find chess really interesting.

When I'd finished talking about art, Mum told me about Ben's latest triumph at chess. Apparently he's got something called a ranking now. Mum proudly told me that he's number twenty-nine in the country for the under-eighteens. She explained how brilliant that was because Ben's only sixteen so he's got nearly two years to raise his position. I couldn't help feeling jealous of my talented big brother. I'd love to be able to raise my position and make my parents proud of me. I sighed. Maybe I would one day.

"And how is your work going, Jessie?"

"Oh…" She'd given me a shock, coming out with that when I thought we were still talking about Ben. "Well, it's okay…"

"It's just that we've had Miss Cardwell on the phone…"

I tensed up instantly and waited to hear what Mum and Dad thought about having a daughter with dyslexia.

"We've heard all about the reading test and everything, and Dad and I are just relieved that at last it looks as though you're going to get some help, Jessie. We never realized what a struggle you've had… Well, we knew you were a slow reader and found spellings hard, but we'd no idea it was such a big problem for you, love. As Miss Cardwell said, the primary school really should have picked up on it. I must say she sounds very nice, Miss Cardwell. Do you get on well with her, Jessie?"

"Yes, she's a really good teacher…I…"

"Dad and I have been saying it's a good thing we

decided on Silver Spires, with its excellent Learning Support department…"

"…and its excellent art department," I quickly added.

"Well, yes… Anyway, Miss Cardwell has put in for an appointment with the educational psychologist, so hopefully we'll get the dyslexia diagnosis confirmed at half-term and then you'll get all the help you need and everything should be a lot easier for you, love."

When I put the phone down I sighed again and wondered whether Mum was picturing me rising up the Year Seven rankings. It annoyed me that she'd been much more focused on my dyslexia than on my art. It was still lovely to talk to her all the same and I couldn't help feeling a bit sad after we'd said goodbye, so it was good that I had something to concentrate on.

Right. Where should I start?

And that was when I realized it was going to take me even longer than usual to google the word *Michelangelo*. It was far too hard to spell and I just had to guess. I was so pleased when the page came up and at the top it said, *Did you mean Michelangelo?* and I saw that I'd spelled it completely wrongly but it didn't matter. They knew what I meant. Then I spent ages trying all the different sites. I'd written down the word *dyslexia* in my sketchbook, so I just kept scrolling down page after page looking out for that word.

But it never appeared. At least, I couldn't see it.

I was feeling really fed up by then and didn't know what to do, and I was also feeling bad because I'd wasted so much time in the computer room and I hadn't done any reading, or, more important by far, any work on my art piece. I decided to google *famous people with dyslexia* and after a couple of shots at the word *famous* it got recognized. But then, hallelujah, there was a list of famous people who were supposed to be dyslexic and amongst the names I found the two I'd been looking for.

It was amazing how happy that made me feel, partly because I'd actually managed to find something on the web all on my own (even if it had taken me ages), but mainly because it looked as though Miss Cardwell wasn't making it up after all. I looked at the other names and saw Albert Einstein. I was certain he was a genius who'd made a fantastic mathematical discovery, so then I felt like dancing round the computer room because I was so happy. This was the proof I needed that having dyslexia really didn't mean you were stupid.

But now I was wondering how I'd ever be able to convince people like Sophie and Isis about that. I sighed. It would be much easier to keep pretending there was nothing the matter. But then there was Grace...and my other friends. Should I tell them the truth? Surely they'd understand. I thought in my heart that they would definitely understand, but then when I remembered Isis and Sophie smirking, my shame came creeping back.

I went back upstairs to the dorm and picked up one of my black bin liners full of wire, then took my precious glass pieces from the back of my drawer and dropped them in the bag. A few minutes later I was in the secret garden and I hadn't passed a soul all the way, because everyone seemed to be out shopping or at the bowlplex.

I started with the smallest figure, the girl, twisting and plaiting wire and shaping it so it would look a bit like a matchstick person. But what was important was the way I arranged the limbs and the head and the back, to get movement in the body. I spent ages moulding it into the position I wanted, as though the figure was looking up at the sky, thinking or maybe daydreaming like I do.

I was so absorbed in my work that I jumped a mile when my mobile bleeped to say I'd got a text.

It was from Katy.

Hows it goin?
Bowling ws gd.
Had pizza etc. Bout 2 go in2
film. C u soon. K x

I don't mind texting because it's taken for granted that you can spell words how you want and everyone can work out what you mean to say anyway. It seemed amazing that Katy and the others had finished bowling and they'd also had a meal. I couldn't believe how much time had gone by. In fact, I suddenly realized I was starving hungry, so I quickly texted Katy back.

Goin ok, hope film is gd
Luv J x

Then I hid my figure under a bin liner, along with the other bin liner of glass pieces and leftover wire, in the narrow space between the hedge and the trees, and went across to the dining hall.

I got a shock as I went in because Grace was sitting there and it was weird that she hadn't texted me to say she was back. Maybe she thought I'd gone to the bowlplex after all. I grabbed my meal and rushed over to find out how she'd got on.

"Not bad," she said, with only a tiny trace of a smile.

My stomach knotted right up because Grace was obviously more upset than I'd thought, and even seemed cross. I felt terrible.

"So what was the score?" I asked brightly, coming out with the first thing that came into my head and realizing immediately that it was a stupid question.

"It's not really to do with scores. It's just which school won the different categories."

I remembered then. "Oh yes, you were in the singles *and* the doubles, weren't you? So...did you... do okay?"

"Yes, Silver Spires won the junior singles and came second in the doubles."

"Oh wow! So that was down to you, Grace! Well done!" I said enthusiastically.

"Thanks," she said. And this time she smiled properly, thank goodness.

I wanted to hang on to this moment while the smile was still there. "Look, I'm really sorry I didn't come along, Grace, I just had so much to do."

Her face softened a bit, but it was like she was making a huge effort, and I'm not used to there being any tension between Grace and me, so it was horrible. "That's okay. How did you get on with your project?"

"I've done the figure of the girl. I think she's going

to look good when she's got some clothes on!"

Grace giggled, and it was such an enormous relief to have her back to normal that I found myself giggling too, but then her face turned serious again.

"Did you...do the work you had to do?" she asked me next.

"Yes...I... Yes."

"So if your work's all done, are you going to the Globe tomorrow then?" she asked, looking at me carefully.

I wished then that I'd not said I'd done my work. I thought about the sheet of paper Miss Cardwell had given me and all the consonant blends we'd worked on together and how determined I was to practise everything she'd shown me in between sessions, so I'd get better and better until my problems disappeared, and a big argument started up from two different places in my brain.

Yes, but Grace will be upset again if you don't go.

I know, but Miss Cardwell won't be very impressed if I haven't done any work on my own and she has to go over the same ground again.

Look, why don't you just explain about your dyslexia to Grace?

No, I can't. It's too embarrassing, and anyway I should have done it in the first place if I was going to.

"I'm really sorry, Grace," I said, giving her that pleading look again, "but if I go to the Globe it'll take up the whole day, and I might not get my... artwork done. I'm really slow at it...trying to get it absolutely perfect...you know."

She nodded slowly but I saw concern in her eyes. "It's okay. I know how much it means to you."

And it was a relief when she tipped her head against mine, like she often did, but I was still confused. I didn't understand what was getting to Grace.

Later, when the others were back and everyone was phoning or e-mailing home, I slipped back to the secret garden to look at my girl figure and collect my bin liner to take back up to the dorm. There was something I wanted to do first though. I reached inside for the crystal teardrops so I could try setting two of them in the circles of wire I'd created for the eye sockets. I just wanted to see what they looked like. I dropped the teardrops on the ground, then stood the figure up against a tree and used the teensiest bit of Blu-tack to lodge the crystals in place. I stood back and took a look, and immediately shivers ran down my spine. The cut glass glinted sharply and somehow brought the figure to life. It was amazing and I was over the moon that I'd had the idea of using the teardrops in the first place. But then I got a shock, because I noticed that on the ground beside the bin liner there were only five pieces of glass in the sparkling pile, and yet I'd definitely collected eight from the room with the old chandelier. Two for each figure. Two of them were in place in my girl figure, which should leave six. Even *I* could work that out.

I rummaged around inside the bag and finally tipped all the remaining wire out of it and searched the whole area around the hedge and the tree carefully, but there was nothing. Not even a glimmer. *I'll have to go back to the room and get another one*, I told myself, *and I'll take more care this time and keep checking that all eight are present and correct.*

The door to the room in the basement opened easily, which was quite a relief because I'd been wondering all the way over what I'd do if it was locked. But then I gasped out loud as a new problem hit me. A much bigger one. The chandelier was gone. Not a single trace of it remained. It had been thrown out already. Now what was I going to do? My whole piece would be spoiled if one of the figures had an eye missing.

I stared at the floor for ages, hoping that a miracle might happen and a teardrop would suddenly magically appear. But eventually I had to stop looking and make my way miserably up to the dorm, my happy, ambitious feelings about the art exhibition slipping and sliding into bleakness, until by the time I'd got to the third floor I'd decided I'd have to leave the eyes out altogether. That thought was so depressing that I began to wonder whether there was any point in carrying on with the art piece at all. How could I have been so careless as to lose something so precious?

But I knew the answer to that perfectly well, and I started punishing myself harshly with the cruellest words, because that was what I deserved.

It's your stupid dyslexic brain, Jess. It even affects your art now.

Chapter Seven

Very gradually, I noticed my reading improving, and that really made me happy. I hadn't had any problems escaping from my friends to go and see Miss Cardwell for my twice weekly sessions either. I think they'd just got used to me going off to work on my project whenever there was a spare moment, because none of them batted an eyelid whenever I said I was going to the secret garden. Not even Grace.

Miss Cardwell was my second favourite teacher now, but Mr. Cary would always be my favourite. I'd told him I was doing a piece of installation art for the exhibition and he'd wanted to hear all about it, but then when I'd explained that I wanted to keep it a secret until it was finished, he'd completely understood.

"Sign of a true artist, Jess! I'm looking forward to seeing it. Any ideas where you're going to install it?"

I shook my head. It was true, I didn't know exactly where would be the best place, except that I wanted my four figures to be surrounding a tree somehow.

If only Mr. Reeves understood me like Mr. Cary did. But he was the complete opposite. He probably thought he was being helpful, but I was growing to dread English lessons because of the things he said to me, and the way people stared.

"Don't worry about spellings, Jessica. It's the content that's important."

Why did he have to say *Jessica*? Now, everyone who wasn't sure before was definitely quite clear that Jessica Roud couldn't spell to save her life.

One day I was sitting in my usual place, roughly in the middle of the room, with Isis and Sophie just behind me. Mr. Reeves was setting us some comprehension work, and as usual he told me not to worry if I couldn't get through it all. "But I'm expecting the rest of you to manage the whole thing," he added, before turning his attention to his laptop. Immediately there was a buzz of noise, but Mr. Reeves was already in his own little world, slapping a CD into the CD player and frowning at the case, too engrossed to tell us to be quiet.

I could have died, but I just sighed inside and tried to settle down to read the mass of words in front of me. A moment later though I felt my face getting hot because Sophie said something to Isis in a voice just loud enough for me to hear.

"Hey, Isis, don't you wish you could do about half the work of everyone else and not even get told off?"

"You're not kidding!"

My throat felt suddenly as though it had something stuck in it and I couldn't swallow. Half of me wanted to turn round and shout and scream, but the other half was scared and cowering. I tried not to move at all. Maybe they'd think I hadn't heard. Everyone else was taking the opportunity to chat with their friends while Mr. Reeves was engrossed with trying to find the right place on a CD, bits of music blasting out every so often, the noise level rising.

I forced myself to try and read the words on the page in front of me instead of just staring at them, but I'd only sounded out half a sentence when Isis's voice made me freeze.

"Hey, Sophie, how about we deliberately make a few spelling mistakes? Then all the teachers will be really nice to us."

That did it. My misery and temper started to roll into one because I was never going to be able to cope in this world of words. Not caring about anything any more, I ripped a page out of my English book and handed it back to Isis. "There you go!" I said in a hiss. "Why not start with those? There are at least three spelling mistakes on every line, because I can't help it. I can't spell. Satisfied?"

I turned away abruptly, feeling my face flooding with colour. It was pathetic, what I'd just said. I was going to be the laughing stock of the class. Why couldn't I have thought of something calm and clever to say that would make them feel small, like Naomi had done?

Around me the class chatted on happily and Mr. Reeves pointed the remote in small impatient jerks at the CD player. Isis and Sophie fell silent behind me but I imagined them rolling their eyes at each other. And when I dared to glance round I saw that no one seemed to have noticed the little pocket of despair where I sat in the middle.

For the rest of that day and for the next two days I don't remember feeling happy at all. Isis and Sophie looked at me as though I was an amusing little child, and although they didn't make any nasty comments in the next English lesson, and didn't come anywhere near me and my friends in the dining hall, I was still tense and anxious. What if they said something to Grace and the others, now they knew for sure that I'd got a big problem?

And if I wasn't replaying that whole horrible English lesson and getting myself worked up all over again, I was trying to think what I could possibly do about the eyes for my art piece. It would be such a shame if this one vital part was missing when I'd worked so hard on the wire bodies. All four of them were finished now, and each figure was made with two strands of wire twisted round into a double, and then three doubles plaited together. It had taken me ages. My girl figure looked incredible, with the bubble wrap in the exact shape of a skirt, and on the top half I'd wrapped the bubble wrap round so it looked like a sweatshirt.

I'd searched again for the missing teardrop but it was obviously lost for good. I was really despairing about what to do until I came across Tony the following day and had the sudden idea of checking with him that the chandelier had actually been thrown away. There was a tiny chance, after all, that it might have been taken somewhere else. I mean it wasn't the kind of thing you could just chuck out with the rubbish; you'd need to arrange for a special collection. Maybe it was being stored somewhere else, ready to be taken away.

Grace and I had been swimming, but Grace had had to stay behind to talk to Mrs. Mellor, the PE teacher, about something. I was waiting outside for her when Tony walked past.

"Can I ask you something?" I blurted out, before I could change my mind.

He turned and grinned at me. "As long as it's nothing to do with maths or English or anything."

"No, it's about...well, you know that room at Hazeldean next to the room where our cases and trunks are stored..."

He stared up at the sky as though he was trying to think where I meant. "Yep, due for decorating, that one," he said, nodding to himself.

"And you know the chandelier in there..."

"Oh, you saw that, did you?" He grinned. "Naughty, naughty! Didn't you read the notice on the door?"

I felt myself blushing as I remembered that there had been words written on a sign on the door but I hadn't tried to read them properly because it would have taken too long. I shook my head, feeling a fool and wondering what the words might have said.

"*Strictly no admission*! Don't think you could have failed to see that!" He was wagging his finger at me, but in a jokey way. "Don't worry, I'll let you off. 'Spect you were just curious…"

At least he wasn't cross, but I was cross with myself. I felt a complete idiot. My terrible reading had let me down yet again. I wasn't sure whether to ask my question now, because a part of me wanted to just get away and put an end to this conversation. But, on the other hand, I'd started off by saying I had a question, so really I had to carry on. "I only poked my head round the door…but I was… wondering whether…er…you've actually chucked the chandelier away yet?"

He looked at me as though I'd just sprouted a horn right in the middle of my forehead. "Chucked it away? *Chucked it away!* You're kidding! That is one precious chandelier, you know. We stored it in there to make sure it was safe. It's been taken away for restoration. It's going to take pride of place in the main reception hall once they've got it back to how it was, with all those bits of glass in place and the whole thing gleaming like twinkle city!" He chuckled to himself, then shook his head as though I was a hopeless case. "Chucked it *away*!"

I was suddenly finding it difficult to swallow. What had I done? I just didn't seem to be able to get anything right. If I'd been able to read the sign I wouldn't have even gone in the stupid room in the first place, but now it looked as though I was a thief as well! They'd get the chandelier to the restorers and find that there were eight pieces of glass missing. I couldn't bear to think about it. I was desperate to ask Tony if they'd have any spare pieces, because I really needed to know whether I was going to be in trouble. But I couldn't ask that question, could I? Or I'd be the – what do you call it in crime films? – yes, the prime suspect. That's what I'd be. I felt my face turning pale.

"What did you want to know for anyway?" asked Tony.

How did I reply to that one? The truth was out of the question. I searched round desperately and my stupid brain actually managed to come up with something.

"I…I thought it would be nice to take a photo of

it, that's all. But it's okay, I'll wait till it's hanging up in the reception hall."

"Ooh, yes, I reckon everyone'll be taking photos once it's hanging up. All that glass. Very expensive, you know."

Maybe this was a chance…if I was very careful. "Yes, it must be. How many pieces of glass are there in it altogether? Or doesn't it matter about having an exact number?"

I held my breath and deliberately let my eyes roam around as though I was just making casual conversation, and the answer wasn't that important to me.

"Oh, it matters, all right! You can't replace all those pieces, you know. Well you could, but it'd cost a bit, and it wouldn't be the same."

Then he was on his way, not a care in the world, while I stood there waiting for Grace and feeling a million cares weighing me down. I must be the most stupid person in the entire world.

Chapter Eight

On Friday evening it was history and science prep. I'd quite like history if it wasn't for all the reading and writing, but I hate science. Georgie and I are in the same set for science and she's no better at it than me, but not for the same reason. The thing about Georgie is that she's just not bothered about any subjects except English and drama, although I've noticed she's recently got keener on French, but that's because she's interested in working on her accent because of her love of acting. I think she might even be planning on taking up another language for GCSE.

I get really worried when I think about things like that. I used to feel okay knowing that Georgie and I were kind of in the same boat, each having one big thing that we're good at. But now she's getting better at other subjects, I feel really anxious that I'm going to be left on my own in bottom sets for ever, because of my brain not working properly.

My eyes went from the mass of meaningless letters in my chemistry book to the door, then back to the book, then back to the door. I was desperately hoping that Grace would arrive. She was having tennis coaching again, just when I needed her. Mia was on the other side of me, but I didn't dare ask her to help me. She'd think I was really thick to not even understand the simplest thing about chemical elements. When I'd had my session with Miss Cardwell earlier on she'd said she could really hear an improvement in my reading, and I'd been so happy. But it wasn't helping me right now, when I couldn't think of the spelling of the simplest word, and I had to keep trying things out on my piece of scrap paper, which would go straight in the bin afterwards.

I felt myself tense up as I remembered what had happened at the end of my session, though, when I'd come out of Miss Cardwell's room. I'd looked to right and left as usual, to check that no one I knew had spotted me, and then I'd had a nasty shock because Isis and Sophie had been at the bottom of the corridor looking at a noticeboard. I'd thought they hadn't seen me, so I'd rushed off in the opposite direction, but I'd hardly gone any distance at all when Isis called out, "Hey, Jess, what are you doing here?"

A ping-pong match seemed to start up inside my brain.

Truth?

Lie?

Truth?

Lie..?

I looked at Isis and suddenly realized she knew exactly what I was doing there. She probably even watched me coming out of Miss Cardwell's room. And she also knew I was embarrassed about it and would probably try to deny it.

That decided it. I stood up straighter and spoke as confidently as possible.

"I've been to Miss Cardwell. I would have thought that was pretty obvious."

They looked at each other, wide-eyed.

Good, I'd shocked them. My heart was beating hard but I felt strong as I turned and walked away, trying with all my might to hold my head up high. "See ya!"

Sitting here in prep, going over that memory, I suddenly felt close to tears. I still hadn't been able to tell the truth to Grace and the others and I was just as ashamed about that as I was about my dyslexia. So why didn't I just tell them and get it over with before they found out from Isis and Sophie?

Was this how little fish in the great big ocean felt? One day, swimming about in the lovely blue sea, and the next, trapped in a net that was tightening and tightening.

Grace didn't arrive till well after halfway through prep, and by that time I'd given up on the chemistry and moved on to history.

"Hi." She smiled as she slipped into her seat and glanced at her watch. A moment later she was hard at work, and in no time at all I saw that she'd covered a page. I knew she wouldn't mind helping me with a few spellings, though, like *Archbishop*, and *Canterbury*, but I didn't want to ask her for spellings like *priest* and *pilgrim* and other words that were simple and obvious for everyone except me.

"You okay?" she mouthed, when she happened to glance around after she'd been scribbling away for another fifteen minutes.

I nodded dejectedly.

"Sure?" She was looking at my work but I quickly

put my arm across it so she couldn't see, because it was so embarrassing.

Immediately that same hurt look came into her eyes – the one I'd seen that lunchtime when I'd been telling her I couldn't come to support her at the tournament. After that she didn't look up any more till the end of prep. She wrote three pages of history altogether, even though she'd had less than half the time I'd had, and I bet there wasn't a single spelling mistake from start to finish.

As soon as my work had been safely handed in so no one could see it, I felt okay to talk about it, and as we went up to the dorm with the others, I tried to sound all light-hearted and unfazed, like Georgie often did. I just wanted Grace to go back to normal.

"I don't think I'll ever get chemical elements, you know!"

"You should have let me help you," Grace said straight away, big concern on her face, and a trace of that hurt look I'd seen earlier.

"Yeah, I could have done with some help too," said Georgie. "Except that I refuse to put any effort into something that is never going to be any use whatsoever in my life. I mean, tell me when I'm going to need to know the chemical symbol for lithium, hmm?"

Everyone was laughing by then, and I envied Georgie so much for the way nothing seemed to bother her.

"I know I'll get into trouble with Miss Crane," she went on brightly, "for not paying attention to her boring, boring lesson yet again, but then if she tried to be a bit more interesting and imaginative, and let us act out little plays all about the elements or something, then who knows, I might be top of the class. So it's entirely her fault!"

One thing I knew for sure was that Miss Crane wouldn't be cross with *me*. None of the teachers were these days. They were all acting like Mr. Reeves, treating me like a little kid. I could get away with the most rubbish piece of work and the teachers were all sympathy and smiles and telling me not to worry, whereas when other people got things wrong, they got accused of not paying attention.

"Anyway, let's not waste time talking about chemistry," Georgie was saying excitedly. "Shopping tomorrow! Yea! I'm going to get a new necklace – a big fat jewel pendant!"

And that gave me a great idea. I knew Grace was quite keen to go on the shopping trip because she needed sweatbands from the sports shop. Perhaps I would go too, because then I could look round for cheap costume jewellery with stones in. It wouldn't even matter if the stones were blue or green, as long as they were big enough to look like eyes. Okay, they wouldn't look as good as the teardrops would have looked, but they'd be better than nothing. I couldn't help myself getting a bit excited again at the thought. But it wasn't enough to mask my worry about what could happen when it's discovered that some pieces of the chandelier are missing.

Grace and I were both wearing jeans for the shopping trip. Normally we dress completely differently from each other. Grace prefers to stick to tracky bums and plain tops and I like experimenting with different styles. I know some people think I'm weird in the way I dress, and I didn't used to care, but now that I'm feeling so like the odd one out with my learning difficulties, I want to blend in as much as possible.

Katy was wearing a really fashionable tunic over her jeans and a belt that she'd made herself. It looked brilliant. She had fabulous earrings on too, and strings of bright beads around her neck. There was nothing interesting about me except perhaps my patchwork shoulder bag that I made myself, which holds my precious camera and goes everywhere with me. Feeling it swinging as I walked along with Grace and the others made me somehow more confident and secure, almost as though the bag had magical properties, and as long as it was close to me I didn't worry so much about my dyslexia. Although it hadn't magicked away my other problem, had it? The small matter of me being a thief. I shivered and clutched it tighter.

There were two minibuses parked not far from Hazeldean, towards the entrance to Silver Spires. Our lovely assistant housemistress, Miss Fosbrook, leaned out of one of them and called to us that the other one was full up. "So fill up this one, now, girls. There should be plenty of room."

She slid back into her seat at the front as Naomi and Katy got in first, then Georgie and Mia, and finally Grace and me. I can remember what happened next as though it was in slow motion. Georgie had plunged ahead of Naomi, straight down to the back and was calling out to the rest of us that there were still a few spaces left there. Naomi and Katy were following with Mia, but Grace turned round to me.

"Shall we sit on our own, Jess?" she asked in her usual quiet voice. "I don't think there are any more seats near the others."

And I opened my mouth to answer but no words

came out, because I'd spotted Miss Cardwell sitting at the front next to Miss Fosbrook. She gave me a huge beaming smile and said, "Hello, Jess! You didn't mention that you were coming on the shopping trip when we had our session yesterday!"

I think that was the moment when the net tightened so strongly that I couldn't move. Grace was staring at me with that look I hated, that I'd seen twice before, only now it was ten times worse. I panicked and felt myself struggling to wriggle my way out of the net as I blurted something about changing my mind, and turned and scrambled down the steps of the minibus. Then I ran and ran in the direction of the secret garden, with tears streaming down my face.

"Jess! Jess!" It was Grace's voice.

My tears came harder. What chance did I have of escaping Grace? She was the fastest runner in Year Seven. And after a while I had to slow down because I was puffed out, and then she slowed down too. I know that because I could hear her footsteps, and anyway she was still saying my name, only more and more weakly, until in the end I was plodding along, head down, seeing only flashes of blurry grey ground through my tears, and hearing nothing now because Grace's footsteps were so light.

"Jess, it doesn't matter..."

I hadn't expected those to be her first words. Subconsciously I was waiting for, "Are you okay?"

I stopped walking and felt her arm go round my shoulders, which just made me start sobbing again.

"It doesn't matter," she repeated.

"Wh...what?" I couldn't manage another word, because my breathing was too gulpy for me to speak properly.

"Let's go and sit down in the secret garden," was all she said.

We walked in silence and I wondered if there was any way I could still get away without mentioning dyslexia, and yet explain why I'd deceived all my friends by never mentioning my visits to Miss Cardwell. But then, there really wasn't any point in hiding anything any more. Even the dyslexia. I may as well just come straight out with the truth. It was definitely going to come out sooner or later. It would be awful and shameful, but I had no choice.

As soon as we sat down on the bench in the secret garden, I started talking in a flat voice.

"I have to go to Miss Cardwell because I can't spell..."

"It doesn't matter."

She didn't get it.

"I mean I can't even spell as well as a little kid in Year Four or something. I've just been pretending. I'm useless at reading and writing and it'll probably take ages before I get any better."

"It doesn't matter."

She really wasn't listening properly.

"I mean I've been going to Miss Cardwell for ages and I didn't tell you because it's embarrassing. But it's worse than just not telling you, I actually lied to you ages ago when Isis and Sophie asked about what Miss Cardwell said. It wasn't because I was ill that I did badly on the test. I lied about that too."

"I know."

How could she have known?

"I don't think you do, Grace." I looked her straight in the eyes. "I'm saying I'm dyslexic – at least, Miss Cardwell's pretty certain I am. It's just got to be confirmed by the educational psychologist at half-term. And that's why I couldn't go to your tennis, because of all the work I had to do. But I didn't blame you for being mad about that – you couldn't have known I was just trying to get better so it wouldn't be quite so embarrassing. Oh yes, and I also couldn't come because I knew it would take me ages on the internet trying to find out if it was true that Michelangelo and Leonardo da Vinci were dyslexic too, because that's what Miss Cardwell said, but I thought she was probably just being kind, and it did take ages because I couldn't even spell their stupid names…"

Suddenly I was exhausted and I just burst into more tears and buried my head in my hands.

"Oh, Jess, please don't cry!" said Grace. "I wasn't cross because you weren't coming to support me at the tournament, I was cross because I *knew* you were going to Learning Support. I mean, at first I knew there was something wrong because you weren't the same you. You were always in daydreams, but it wasn't like your usual daydreams, when you're picturing things. These were different daydreams, and at times I just felt as though I'd lost you. There was something about the way you always looked down when you said you were going to work on your art, and I could tell you weren't telling the truth, so I followed you one day and I saw where you went…"

I gasped when Grace said that, and it was as though my face didn't know whether to turn white or red. "I didn't know you knew…"

"But I wanted you to tell me yourself. I was so upset because you weren't confiding in me, and I thought I must be a rubbish best friend if you couldn't even tell me you had to have learning support and then you wouldn't let me help you in prep."

"But it's worse than learning support, it's *dyslexia*!" I said, through sobs.

Now it was Grace's turn to look straight at me. She even raised her voice. "But I've told you, it doesn't matter! It doesn't change what you've always been, it's just got a title now. It's nothing to do with how intelligent you are or anything like that. Surely Miss Cardwell explained that? I know all about it, Jess, because, the thing is, my big sister, Sunisa, is dyslexic too."

I gasped again. A bigger gasp than before. "Oh!" There was a silence. I couldn't find the words to show how relieved I was.

"It's not made you stop liking your sister, has it?" I finally mumbled.

And that's when Grace burst into tears and *I* had to put my arm round *her*. "Oh I'm sorry, Grace. I didn't mean to upset you. I was just so ashamed of myself for being so bad at easy things like reading and writing."

Grace stopped crying and looked at me through her tears. "Jess, how can I get it through to you that it's *not* bad. You mustn't keep thinking of it as a bad thing. My sister says that some people don't get it at first, but they always do in the end. Like this girl who used to mock her in class, and was always saying snidey things about her under her breath... Well, one day, the teacher told this girl to remove her glasses, because she wore glasses for reading, and the girl did as she was told, and the teacher asked her to read something from her book, and the girl said, 'I can't see the words without my glasses,' and the teacher said, 'Well, now you know what it's like for Sunisa. Your brain can't read the words without help, and neither can Sunisa's.' And from that day on, the girl stopped her taunting. She just hadn't realized till then that actually she was in the same boat as Sunisa. And now they're at uni and they're the best of friends."

I'd completely stopped crying during Grace's story and so had she. The two of us looked at each other, with our tear-stained faces and red eyes, and I don't know which one of us saw the funny side of it first, but the next minute we were laughing our heads off, until we got into that hysterical state you get into when you just can't stop.

Grace was the first to recover. "Can I see your art piece now, Jess?" she asked.

I only hesitated for a second. Then I went behind the hedge and pulled out my metal figures and stood them up against the trees.

"Oh wow! They look amazing, Jess! Totally amazing!"

"Really?" I was pleased and surprised, because to me they looked incomplete, as where the teardrops should have been there were just rings of wire with nothing inside.

"Don't you think they look like...there's something missing, Grace?"

She shook her head slowly with a frown on her face. "No, I think they're perfect."

We talked so much, Grace and I, that afternoon, making plans about how much she would help me – in fact how all my friends would help me, and about what we'd actually say to them to explain why I'd run off.

"I think you've just got to tell the truth, Jess. These are your friends we're talking about. Of course they'll understand."

I nodded. Grace had definitely made me feel stronger. She'd helped lift my confidence, and I *would* tell the truth because she was right, the truth was the only way.

Except for one little truth.

Grace still didn't know that, as well as being dyslexic, her best friend was also a thief.

Chapter Nine

Later that afternoon, when the others were back from shopping, Grace called a friendship meeting. We all sat round in our dorm on the circular mat and talked and talked. It was a bit embarrassing at first because everyone looked so serious and anxious. Even Georgie was throwing wide-eyed worried looks all over the place. The weird thing was that when I told them all that it was pretty much definite that I'd got dyslexia and I'd been keeping it a secret because I was ashamed of it, there was a pause before anyone spoke and I could see puzzled looks appearing on all their faces. Naomi was the first to say anything.

"But why were you ashamed? Surely you were pleased, because it explains everything. It's totally the reason why you find it hard to read and write."

Then the others all started agreeing and saying there was nothing wrong with being dyslexic, it was no different from being left-handed. I began to think I must have been totally crazy to have ever worried about what my friends would say when they found out. They'd made it all sound so simple and obvious. If only I'd told them ages before.

It felt like the end of the meeting and we were all just about to get up when there was a tap on the door and in came Miss Fosbrook. "We've just been talking about my dyslexia," I told her quietly.

"And we think it's no big deal!" added Georgie firmly, as Grace held my hand for a moment.

Miss Fosbrook squashed herself into our circle and gave me a big hug. She's only in her early twenties and she's really popular at Hazeldean because she almost seems like one of us students.

"Listen, Jess," she said, patting my knee, "I was talking to Miss Cardwell on the shopping trip, and I'm sure you don't need me to say anything when you've got all these brilliant friends, but I just wanted you to know that everyone's rooting for you, and you're not the only one in this school with dyslexia. Miss Cardwell's going to arrange to get you hooked up with a couple of older girls who you can chat to. Then you'll feel better." She flashed me a big beam as she stood up and reached into her jeans pocket. "That reminds me, Miss Cardwell asked me to give you this."

It was a card with a picture of a little ant with a rucksack on its back, looking anxiously up at a hill it was about to climb. Inside, Miss Cardwell had written, "You, of all people, can climb this hill, Jess! It's not half as bad as it seems. Looking forward to seeing you on Monday."

I put the card on the pinboard above my bed. I thought it would be good to look at if ever I'm feeling depressed. It'll remind me of this day and how all my worries fell away.

Well nearly all.

It was two days later in assembly when Ms. Carmichael, the Head of the whole school, said she had an important announcement to make.

"You are all aware that there is a great deal of new building and restoration work going on in the school, girls, which is all very exciting. There is, however, a small hitch which has come to our notice, and this is where I need your help."

My knees trembled and I dreaded what I was certain was coming.

"We took the chandelier down from the old library building, as it needed cleaning and a considerable amount of restoration, and it's been stored in an empty room in the basement of Hazeldean boarding house…"

The whole assembly hall was still and silent, hanging on Ms. Carmichael's every word. It felt like such a big build-up, as though she was telling a story and everyone was dying to know what happens in the end. I could feel the tension all around me, and the more she went on, the more I wondered how I was going to be able to hide my guilt. It was probably written all over my face already.

"Now, the hundreds of little glass pieces that make up the chandelier are very precious and individual, so when it was taken down, the men were careful to check that there weren't any pieces missing…" Ms. Carmichael paused as her eyes flew round the hall. "And there weren't…" Another pause while my stomach turned over. "And yet the restorers have phoned to say that there are eight pieces of glass missing. So if anyone has found them, or happens to see them, please come to either myself or your housemistress. Obviously the sooner we get the pieces back, the sooner we can have our precious chandelier hanging up in reception. So let's all keep our eyes peeled."

She finished with one of those smiles that isn't really a smile because there's too much sadness in it, and then we all filed out and I felt my head bursting with terrible guilty thoughts and questions.

Why hadn't Ms. Carmichael come straight to me? She must have talked to Tony about the chandelier and the missing pieces because he would have been in charge of moving it to the room at Hazeldean. So why didn't Tony tell her that one of the girls had been in the room? I know I only said I wanted to take a photo of it, but surely he would have reported that to Ms. Carmichael. After all, I even asked him how many pieces there were.

All through that day I worried about what to do. I knew what I *ought* to do. I ought to hand the seven pieces in, admit that I'd made a terrible mistake and apologize like mad that I'd lost the last piece. But what would happen to me? Could you get expelled for something like that?

By the time it came to my lunchtime session with Miss Cardwell I was in a terrible state. My friends could tell that there was something wrong, but they all thought I was getting myself worked up about having to face Miss Cardwell after acting so dramatically and bursting into tears and everything the last time I'd seen her.

Half of me wanted to spill my troubles out to Grace, but now I was stuck worrying about what she'd think of me, all over again. My dyslexia might not be my fault, but taking bits of school property and losing one of them definitely was, and I just couldn't face having to make any more embarrassing admissions to Grace.

By the end of school I was a wreck and I went to the secret garden to work on my figures in the hope that it might make me feel better. But it didn't. In fact it made me feel worse.

They were almost complete now. Mr. Cary had watched me stippling acrylic paint onto the bubble wrap for a suit for the figure of the woman, even though I hadn't told him what it was for.

"I'm intrigued, Jess. It's such an original material to be using. I can't wait to see your finished artwork."

He'd given me a piece of card to write about my installation on and I'd waited for him to say something like, "Don't worry about spellings", because I was so used to all the teachers talking to me like that. But all he'd said was, "Name, title of piece and brief explanation, okay?"

I smiled to myself now as I stood back to see the effect of my four figures propped up against a tree. I liked the way they were facing north, south, east and west. It somehow symbolized the different way each of them looked at the world. But then when I'd been standing there perfectly still for a while, just staring, I started to feel as lifeless and pointless as the metal figures in front of me. I sighed a massive sigh and put my head in my hands, then abruptly opened my eyes and felt furious with myself for not even managing to finish them off properly. And the more I looked, the more my temper rose. They were useless without the eyes. Useless. And suddenly I couldn't bear the sight of them for another second.

I grabbed the woman and the girl and started to walk off towards the rubbish dump, but I'd hardly taken two steps when I practically bumped into Grace.

"Jess! What's the matter? What are you doing?"

I felt trapped. I gulped and spoke in a whisper, feeling my shoulders hunching up like a little girl's.

"I can't tell you. I mean, this time I really can't. I've done something unforgivable."

"Oh, Jess, not this again. If I'm your best friend you've got to tell me. If I'm not, then…you needn't bother."

"You'll hate me."

"If it turns out that I hate you, I'll give you every single last coin of the money that Mum and Dad have put in savings for me." She stuck out her hand. "Shake on it."

So we did, and I told her. Just like that. All in one long garbled sentence.

"It was me who took the pieces of chandelier for my art project, only I lost one of them and I still can't find it, but I didn't realize it was precious and going to be repaired, I thought it was going to be chucked out and I didn't think it mattered, and I couldn't read what it said on the door because of my useless brain and now everything's useless and I'm not entering the art exhibition and I'll probably get expelled and I bet you hate me."

I'd delivered my whole speech staring at the ground and I still didn't dare look up at Grace.

"Oh, Jess, you made a mistake, that's all. You've simply got to hand the pieces in and explain that you couldn't read the notice and that will be that!"

I looked up then. I couldn't believe that Grace was taking it all so calmly. Anyone'd think I'd just told her I'd borrowed her hairdryer or something and put it back in the wrong place. She didn't look shocked at all. But she'd forgotten one small detail.

"There are only seven pieces, remember," I said in scarcely more than a whisper.

"So we find the eighth one." Then she suddenly frowned at what I was carrying. "Where were you going with your art, Jess?"

"To the rubbish dump. Can you get the other two figures for me? I can't carry them all."

"Oh, Jess, please don't do this to yourself."

But I just started striding off again because I was determined to finally get rid of the useless old metal and bubble wrap. I didn't know why I'd ever thought it was anything special. "I'm doing myself a favour," I called back over my shoulder.

Grace hurried after me with the other two figures, and it was a relief to chuck them all away. But a few minutes later we were back at the secret garden, because Grace said she wanted to go all over the area where I'd been working with a fine-tooth comb.

"I'm sure that missing piece must be here somewhere." Those were the only words she'd said for a while. I think she was more upset than *I* was about me throwing my art away, although I had felt a stab of sadness when I'd looked back and seen the four figures lying there on the dump, staring up at the sky with their sightless eyes.

Grace crouched down and peered at the earth. Then she looked up quickly to tell me to go back and double-check in the dorm. I suddenly felt drained and was really glad that she was taking charge, but there was one thing I had to be sure of.

"Do you think I might get expelled?"

She jumped to her feet like a jack-in-the-box. "Course you won't! Don't be silly, Jess! Honestly! Oh and keep your eyes on the ground on the way back to Hazeldean. We've got to be thorough."

There was no one in the dorm, thank goodness, because no way was I going to tell any of the others about my stupidity. This would stay between Grace and me, unless it turned out that I did get expelled – then everyone would find out anyway.

I ran my fingers over every bit of floor under my bed, and under everyone else's just for good measure. Then I looked in all my drawers, even though I knew there was no way the glass piece could have got in there, and finally I walked very slowly back to the secret garden, head down, scouring the ground all the way.

"Any luck?" asked Grace in a small voice when I reappeared.

I shook my head. There was no point in asking her the same question. It was obvious she hadn't found anything. But then, very slowly, she held out her tightly closed hand and uncurled her fingers one at a time. When I saw the crystal winking up at me, I screeched "Yesssss!" at the top of my voice, and Grace hugged me tight.

"I had to scrape up loads of soil," she said, breaking off the hug. "Look at my disgusting black nails!"

I thanked her about a million times as I put this last missing teardrop with the others and we jogged back to Hazeldean together on our way to see Miss Carol. When we were almost there Grace broke into a giggle. "Sorry I tricked you," she said. "I couldn't resist it!"

I laughed. "That's okay." Surprisingly I didn't feel at all nervous any more now I'd got all eight pieces of glass, though I couldn't help tensing up when we stood outside Miss Carol's flat. "You will come in with me, won't you?" I whispered.

"Course I will," said Grace. And without hesitation I knocked on the door.

"Come in and sit down girls," said Miss Carol,

a welcoming smile on her face as always. "What can I do for you?"

I took a deep breath and held out my hand with the eight crystals. I was watching her carefully and her eyes were out on stalks. "Oh!" She seemed stuck for words. "Wh...where did you find them?"

And that was the first moment that it ever occurred to me that I needn't have worried about being expelled or anything because if I wanted I could simply tell a lie.

In the long grass at the side of the athletics field.

Amongst the rhododendrons that line the drive.

In the laundry room.

There were so many possible lies I could tell, but I knew it would be stupid to tell any of them, so I told the truth. And I finished off by saying, "I'm really sorry. I know I should have spent more time trying to read the notice on the door in the basement, but I was so excited about my art project..."

Miss Carol leaned forwards and patted my hand. "It was brave of you to hand them in, Jess."

"Will you...will you tell Ms. Carmichael it was me?"

She nodded. "Yes, I will, but Ms. Carmichael won't need to share that information with anyone else, so don't worry."

I thanked her, and Grace and I got up to go a few minutes later. But when we were almost out of the door, Miss Carol suddenly said, "So what exactly were you going to use the glass for?"

"Oh, just something for my art project, but it doesn't matter. I'm not even entering the art exhibition now."

"Oh dear, that's a shame. Why is that?"

I shrugged. "I don't like the piece I've done any more."

Miss Carol frowned and repeated that it was a shame, then we all said goodbye and that was that. The dreaded deed was done and I felt so much better.

"Are you double-certain about not entering the art exhibition, Jess?" Grace asked me as we walked over to supper.

"Yes," I said, my crossness flaring up again. "The figures aren't right without eyes. They're not how I imagined them."

"You're not just kind of...punishing yourself?" Grace said then.

I hesitated because I didn't know what she meant, then shook my head firmly and said, "No. I don't want people looking at my art when I can't bear to look at it myself." Then inside my head, with a heavy sadness, I added, *Especially not Brian Hodgson.*

"Sure?" Grace tried again, quietly.

"Double-positive."

And she gave up after that.

Chapter Ten

None of my friends could persuade me to change my mind about the art exhibition. They all looked at me as though I was totally mad when I just kept shrugging and said I simply wasn't bothered about it any more.

"But I don't get why you've changed your mind," said Georgie. "I mean, what's different now from when you first started the project?"

"I just don't think the figures look as good as I'd imagined they'd look, and I don't like entering something that's less than perfect."

"Would you let us see them?" asked Naomi.

I hesitated and Grace jumped in.

"I think it would be good if the others saw them," she said quietly. Then she turned her palms up, as a look of complete bewilderment came over her face. "You'll all think she's crazy not to enter when you see the brilliant work she's done."

A picture of my friends staring at the figures on the rubbish dump came into my head, and I tensed up at the thought of them all racking their brains to try and think of something nice to say to make sure I wouldn't be upset.

"No, they're not worth seeing, honestly. And anyway, I've chucked them away, so that's the end of that."

Then later I had the terrible task of going to tell Mr. Cary what I'd decided.

"Ah, Jess!" he said, with a smile as I approached him. "Come to give in your card?"

"Er...no...actually..."

His smile dissolved into a look of big concern. "What's up, Jess?"

I took a deep breath and sucked my lips in tight, quickly practising the words I'd prepared, then I spoke them in a rush. "I've decided not to enter because I don't like what I've done. It's not...right."

Mr. Cary shook his head slowly. "No, no, no,"

he said quietly. "That's just an artist's thing, Jess. You work and work on something and after a while you can't see it objectively any more and it doesn't feel fresh and original and you start to have doubts. Really…"

"No, it's not that. I just know it's rubbish…"

"Well why don't you let me be the judge of that. I won't push you into entering if you really don't want to, but I'm sure I'll be able to see something in your work that you can't see yourself because you're just too close to it."

"It won't make any difference. I just don't want to enter it."

He shook his head again and I could tell he was really sad. "Have you filled in the card?"

"I didn't see the point."

"Okay, Jess, just do that one thing for me. Just fill in the card. Write whatever you would have written."

I shrugged. I didn't really get why Mr. Cary wanted me to do that. He was still looking at me so I shrugged again and said, "All right."

He looked carefully at me then. "I need you to promise to do the card for me, Jess."

I didn't understand why he was so insistent. What was he going to do with it?

"I promise…as long as you chuck it away when you've looked at it."

He sighed and gave me a sad smile. "You drive a hard bargain, Jess." Then he glanced behind me because Katy was rushing in, flapping her card.

"I've done it."

"Excellent, Katy. Go and display it next to your jewellery."

But Katy turned to me instead, with pleading eyes and praying hands. "Please, *please* change your mind, Jess."

"What are we going to do with her?" Mr. Cary asked Katy, folding his arms and tipping his head on one side.

"I don't know. We all think she's totally mad," said Katy, grabbing my shoulders and looking urgently into my eyes. "Just think about how exciting tomorrow afternoon is going to be, Jess, when Brian Hodgson judges the exhibition, and we get the afternoon off to look round all the art…"

That weight of sadness came over me again. I'd so wanted Brian Hodgson to look at my work. But then I imagined him and everyone else looking at my sightless figures and felt more sure than ever that I was doing the right thing.

"There's the big barbecue, remember?" went on Katy, ignoring my silence.

"And the parents will get to see the art in the second half of term when it's open day." Mr. Cary took up the trying-to-get-Jess-to-change-her-mind talk.

I tried to imagine Mum and Dad and Ben looking round the school. If I'd won a prize I knew they'd be really proud of me. But then there was no way I was going to win a prize with four unfinished figures, was there? So I didn't know why I was even thinking about that.

"Sorry," I said, firmly to Mr. Cary. I didn't want to look at his face again, so I just turned to leave. "Sorry."

For the rest of the day I kept on going over the conversation I'd had with Mr. Cary. I could tell he was genuinely sad that I wasn't entering and that made me sad too. I kept on thinking what to write on the card, but whatever I wrote would be pointless because I didn't believe in my work any more. I should never have agreed to do it. It was so much harder than I'd thought it would be.

By the time we all went to bed I still hadn't done

it, but then I couldn't get to sleep for thinking about it. It was as though the stupid art exhibition was haunting me, not letting me forget it.

In the end I sat up in bed and snapped on my little bedside light, not even caring whether I was disturbing the others. I glanced round quickly and saw that they were all asleep anyway, so I hung over the edge of the bed and reached down to grab the card and a pencil from my desk below. Then I stared at the card for a while, getting myself worked up into a temper because absolutely no words would come. I folded my arms crossly and squeezed my eyes tight to make a picture of those stupid figures on the rubbish dump come up in my mind. Then I started scribbling furiously...

This is a bunch of peaple on the rubish heap who cant see proply.

Why cant they see? Becase stupid Jessica Roud did'nt manidge to sort out any eyes for them. Why did'nt she manidge such a simple thing? Becase she cant even read. The end.

I tucked the card under my pillow, snapped off my light and curled up tight under the duvet. I might have promised Mr. Cary that I'd give him the card, but I didn't say when, did I? The next day he was sure to be flat out making sure everything was in place for the exhibition, and looking after Brian Hodgson, so there was no way he'd think about my card. And he wouldn't be interested in what I'd written once the exhibition was over, would he? Good. I'd done what he wanted me to do. I'd kept my part of the bargain.

And now I could go to sleep.

After lunch the following day, the whole school seemed to start buzzing. Everyone was rushing in all directions, including us. But I felt peculiar. Half of me loved seeing all the art, but the other half felt like a ghost at a party. I used to be a part of all this happiness and excitement but now I wasn't, and it hurt a bit.

It was as though a sorcerer had been weaving magic at Silver Spires during lunchtime, because we kept on coming across pieces of art everywhere we looked. There were wind chimes made of pottery that hung in trees, and a little garden in the patch of land in front of the science lab, filled with ceramic mushrooms and toadstools. There were even gargoyles attached to outbuildings, that looked as though they'd been cut out of breeze blocks and painted in bright acrylic colours. One of them was amazing. I studied the little plaque beside it and saw that it was a Year Nine girl who'd made it.

In the shrubbery near the tennis courts was a shelter made of twigs and stones and wood, with an incredible curtain of leaves. I'd watched the shelter develop over the last few days, but the girl who did it must have made her curtain of leaves somewhere else and just hung it up today. She was in Year Nine too.

"Look, she's called it 'Hidden'," said Naomi. "I like that idea."

Her big eyes stared into the distance and I had the sudden jolting feeling that she might appreciate my family of figures. But I quickly pushed the thought away, because it was too late now, and anyway I'd promised myself I wouldn't think about it any more, I'd just concentrate on enjoying the sight of all the other art.

"*Please* can we see your jewellery now?" I begged Katy for the twentieth time.

Naomi was as desperate as me. "Come on, Kates," she said. "We've seen just about everything else."

"All right," said Katy, grinning. "Follow me!"

She led us to the art block, then stopped dramatically and folded her arms, looking at us with shining, challenging eyes. "Bet you can't find it!"

"What?" said Georgie. "Course we'll find it. It'll be with the rest of the jewellery, won't it?"

"You'll just have to see," said Katy mysteriously. "But don't rush round. Look at everything carefully. That's the only clue I'm giving you."

I felt glad that Katy had told us to take our time, because there was so much to see. The art block was totally transformed. It always looked great, but today it looked breathtaking. There were murals and ceiling paintings, stained-glass windows and corridors turned into underwater tunnels with sea life surrounding you as you walked along. There were ceramic pots and jugs and animals and birds, and hats made of feathers and felt; there was every style of picture and photograph, small and large and gigantic, using every type of material and technique under the sun.

"Oh wow!" Georgie made us all come and look at what was on a table all on its own. "I want this!"

It was a silver necklace on a plaster-of-Paris bust, only it didn't just go round the neck, it hung in strands right round the shoulders like the tassles of a scarf. It was truly beautiful.

"Yes, I know," said Katy, pouting, pretending to be fed up. "This is so going to win a prize, and don't worry, guys, I know my bracelet won't get anywhere, but I loved making it and I can't wait till you see it."

We still hadn't found it and I was getting more and more intrigued.

"Look at this wall, Jess," said Naomi. "There are some lovely pictures here."

"Yes, this one's…" I stopped and gasped. I was staring at a black sheet of A3 paper with silver bracelets of all sorts of different designs painted all over it, only one of them wasn't painted. It was real. And on the bottom right-hand corner were Katy's initials, *K.P.*

"Wow, Kates!" said Naomi, swinging round and hugging Katy, who was grinning from ear to ear. "It's amazing!"

"Oh, Katy," I breathed. "It's…" I was searching for the right word and it popped into my head in next to no time. "It's exquisite!"

"Thank you, Jess! That's a really big compliment because of you being such an artist."

I felt a tightness in my stomach. Could I still count myself as an artist when I'd just chucked away my latest piece of art?

Grace squeezed my hand. Maybe she'd noticed my sad look. "Let's look at everything all over again," she whispered. "We've got an hour till the judging."

So that's what we did, only this time we stopped and read all the little plaques – at least the others did, and Grace read them out loud for me. It was such a lovely relief not having to worry any more about not being able to read when I was with my friends.

At three o'clock everyone assembled on the lawn on the other side of the drive that scooped past the main building. I looked up and saw the tall thin spires spraying sparkles into the bright sunny sky, and when I looked back down again Mr. Cary and the other art teachers were approaching the platform on the lawn from the art block, with a tall slim-looking man. He had short silver hair and was wearing a loose white shirt, grey trousers, a black waistcoat with yellow braiding round it, and a thin chain round his neck. My heart beat faster. This was Brian Hodgson.

Everyone cheered like mad when Mr. Cary introduced him and he grinned round, and said, "What a welcome! Thank you! And what a lovely school with talent sprouting everywhere. I think you should be very proud of yourselves." There was more cheering then. "I've had great difficulty choosing my winners and my two runners-up in each category," he went on in a more serious tone, "but I've finally managed it. I'd like to start with the senior category, if I may, simply because the three winning entries are within ten metres of me."

We all started looking round but there was nothing to be seen within ten metres of where we were standing, so I was a bit confused.

Brian reached down and took something out of a large canvas bag. "Here is the work of the second runner-up," he announced, turning it round with a flourish to face us. "Would Tessa Phillips please come and receive her prize?"

Tessa was in Year Eleven and she'd done the most brilliant illustration for a children's book. She'd used a photograph for the background and painted cartoon characters on the top. It was atmospheric and amazing and I clapped like mad along with everyone else as she shook Brian's hand and he gave her an envelope.

When she left the platform, we all fell quiet and Brian began to speak again. "Now I said that all the winning entries in this category could be seen within ten metres of where we are standing and you all dutifully looked round, but no one thought to look up."

So then of course the entire school looked up at the old oak tree, since there was no other place where the artwork could be, and, sure enough, half hidden by leaves and hanging between two branches was a great brown bat, that looked as though it was made of the finest spun silk. It wasn't just the bat that was so impressive, it was the way the artist had thought to camouflage it like that.

A girl called Helena went to collect the first runner-up prize for the bat as the applause rang round, and then everyone was still and silent, waiting to hear who had won the senior category.

"This might not come as a surprise to any of you," Brian announced with a grin, as he carefully took from his canvas bag the plaster-of-Paris bust with the silver necklace draped around it. "Congratulations to Ayesha Gala!"

Katy nodded and whispered, "Told you!" as Ayesha got an even bigger round of applause than the other two. I noticed that Brian was mouthing something to Mr. Cary, who nodded and gave him a thumbs up.

"Good," said Brian, when we were all quiet again. "We're ready for the junior category. I have a confession to make. I couldn't decide who should be runner-up number two and who should be runner-up number one in this category, so I'm having a joint runners-up prize. First, let me show you this magnificent mosaic of cut glass, every single shape melted in a kiln by Celine Farrier and placed in the most beautiful pattern." He held up the mosaic for us all to see and I felt happy that it was a winner because I'd guessed it might be when I'd spotted it in the art block. Where did Celine get the glass from? Maybe she'd just asked for it. Why hadn't I done that? I was so stupid.

After Celine had received her prize, Brian said he was sorry but he couldn't whip the other runner-up's entry out of his bag, because it was far too big, and neither could we look around and see it because it was too far away. "But," he went on, "if I were to say the word 'Hidden', what would spring to mind?"

Georgie's voice rang out loud and clear. "That tree house thingy!"

There was instant laughter and when it died down Brian chuckled and said he thought *"That tree house thingy"* didn't quite do it justice, but yes, that was the other runner-up. "So, many congratulations to Claudia Driver!"

I was trying to work out in my mind who would be the overall winner of the junior category. It would have been so amazing if it was Katy, but I guessed that Brian wouldn't choose two pieces of jewellery.

Maybe it would be that fabulous gargoyle.

"And finally, the winner of this junior section." Again, the rustling and chatting dissolved into a deep silence.

"Now, many of you might not have even seen this winning entry as you've been looking round today, but I'm sure you'll all go and see it once I tell you about it. I didn't see it myself at first because it's way over there..." He pointed. "Near the place where you keep your pets." He paused and grinned round, and then a murmur went round the audience. "But Mr. Cary pointed me in the right direction and I found myself at the school rubbish dump..."

I felt a gasp rising up inside me and I swung round to look at Grace, but she was staring straight ahead, her shoulders tensed right up.

"On the rubbish dump were four figures made of twisted wire and dressed fantastically in painted bubble wrap. They were lying there as though they'd been chucked off the edge of the world, and I can honestly say that the sight of those figures, who seemed to be staring tragically up into the sky, had more effect on me than any piece of art I've seen for a very long time."

My throat felt tight and tears were coming into my eyes. Grace stood closer to me and I saw that her face had gone a bit red, but she kept her eyes straight ahead, and I did the same because Brian was carrying on.

"I'd like to read you what was written on the plaque beside this piece of art."

He produced a card from his pocket and I bit my lip, my heart thumping fearfully as Brian's voice rang out. "This is a bunch of people on the rubbish heap who can't see properly. Why can't they see?"

My hand shot to my mouth. *No! Don't read any more. I can't bear it.* These were the words I'd written in a big temper. But then I realized Brian had stopped reading and he was looking round his audience very slowly. "That's all it says," he announced finally. "And that is part of the genius of the piece. *Why can't they see?* The artist has left the audience to give whatever meaning they want to these frail wire people. I have my own feelings about it, but...they may not be the same as the artist's. And that, ladies and gentlemen, is the beauty of art. There *is* no right or wrong!" He smiled round and I felt shivers rushing all over me. It was like a dream. Perhaps I *was* dreaming. Perhaps I would wake up any minute now and plummet into my real world.

A murmur was rippling through the audience. *But who won? Who did it? Who's the winner?*

And then my name was announced and I realized it definitely wasn't a dream because I was being shoved forwards by my friends as everyone else clapped and cheered.

"Go on!" whispered Grace.

"You total genius!" squeaked Katy.

I felt hands patting me on the back and the shoulders and the arms as I tried to find a path through the crowd. "Congratulations!" "Well done, Jessica!" "Brilliant!"

And then Isis's voice, loud and clear. "You're so clever, Jess. Well done!"

I was gobsmacked, and fully expected to see a mocking look on her face, but when our eyes met I saw something I'd never seen in Isis before. It was real admiration, and I walked on air all the rest of the way to the front, where Brian Hodgson's big friendly smile seemed to guide me right up to him. As we shook hands, with the clapping and cheering and whooping and whistling going on all around us, Brian gave me a thoughtful look. "You've got a rare talent there, Jessica. Take great care of it, won't you?"

I nodded and smiled. I *would* take great care of it.

Brian had convinced me that I wasn't completely useless at everything. I might be no good with words, but I had enough artistic talent to be praised by a great artist – and that was something to be truly proud of.

Then he handed me an envelope and wished me the best possible luck for the future. "Not that you'll need it. You're a rising star," he added, which made my heart sing as I walked on air again, back to my friends. By the time I got there the clapping had finally faded and people were starting to move away.

"Look, everyone's gone to look at your art, Jess," said Naomi, clapping her hands together like a little girl. "See you in a minute!"

And that was when I started to step out of my dream and to wonder what on earth had happened to bring my card into Brian Hodgson's hands. The last time I'd seen it was just before I'd put it under my pillow. I just didn't get it.

As soon as Grace and I were completely on our own I swooped on her. "I don't understand what happened with my card!"

She bit her lip. "I...I saw you writing something last night in bed, because I was wide awake, only I pretended to be asleep. And I saw you put whatever it was under your pillow, and I could tell you were in a state. So this morning when you went to the bathroom I took it out and read it, and it made me sad… In fact, it made me so sad that I was suddenly determined to do something about it."

I gasped. "But what about my terrible spelling?"

"It's okay. I got the first two sentences in my head, then I rubbed out the whole thing and wrote out just those first two sentences so they filled up the card nicely. Are you…cross?" She looked as though she was holding her breath, waiting for my reply, and it suddenly hit me that she was the very best possible best friend in the world.

I gave her a hug and felt the tears at the backs of my eyes again. "No, of course not. How could I be cross? I've just won the exhibition, thanks to you."

"When I went to Mr. Cary at morning break and said you'd changed your mind, he looked as though he didn't believe me and I went red and suddenly found myself telling him the truth – I mean the whole truth, about everything. I hope…you don't mind. Then I handed him the card and said you'd written it after lights out. I didn't tell him I'd changed it a bit."

My hand went to my mouth in horror. "Wh… what did he say?"

"He asked me to show him your piece and I took him to the rubbish dump and he just stared and stared. He had tears in his eyes and he asked me where I thought we should put the card, and I said 'What, so we're leaving the figures here? I think Jess wanted them to lean against a tree looking out in all four directions.' And he said, 'No, what Jess wanted in the end was to chuck them on this rubbish heap. So that is exactly where we'll leave them.' Then he took the card and placed it really carefully between the fingers of the smallest figure."

Grace put her arm round me. "I told the others what I'd done at lunchtime, because I couldn't bear to be the only one keeping such a massive secret!" She smothered a nervous giggle. "They couldn't believe it. Georgie called me a black horse, until Naomi pointed out that she actually meant *dark* horse!"

I laughed then. It was a big spluttery laugh of relief and joy.

Grace grabbed my hand. "Come on, Jess. Let's go and join the others to look at your piece."

We jogged all the way and I couldn't believe that so many people were still congregated around the rubbish dump.

"Aha! Here's the artist!" said Brian, seeing us approaching. "There are a lot of people here wanting to be put out of their misery, Jessica. Everyone wants to know what *you* think is the answer to your question *'Why can't they see?'*"

I spotted Naomi and Katy and Mia at that moment and they all looked at me with waiting, wondering eyes, and then Georgie was grinning at me, and Grace shuffled a bit closer to me, and I suddenly realized how lucky I was to have these special friends, and also how silly I was ever to have thought they wouldn't stand up for me no matter what I'd done. And on the other side of the rubbish dump stood Mr. Cary. Our eyes met and he broke into a big smile as he gave me a thumbs up and a little nod.

"They couldn't see because they had their eyes closed," I answered firmly, "but I think they're open again now."

Mr. Cary moved round towards me and Brian. "In which case," he said in his announcer's voice for all to hear, "we must move them off this rubbish dump and find the perfect place for them at Silver Spires."

"What about the reception hall?" came Miss Carol's voice from somewhere amongst the crowd. "They'll look wonderful with those sparkling lights shining on them!"

"What do *you* think, Jess?" asked Mr. Cary.

"I think that would be perfect," I replied, feeling the little private light inside me glowing more brightly than surely even the chandelier, with all its teardrops, could ever glow.

And at that same moment, Grace and I exchanged a look.

A best friends' look, that said more than a thousand words.

School Friends Fun

I love being at Silver Spires — not only are my best friends here, but with all the activity and excitement it's the perfect place for capturing cool arty images, which look fab on my pinboard. Why not try snapping pics of your friends to decorate your room too?

Getting snap happy!

I carry my camera everywhere I go, to make sure I never miss that perfect photo opportunity. Sometimes the most interesting images come from the most unexpected places – half the fun is finding them! Here are my top tips for stunning photos.

★ Try taking pics at the eye level of your subject – so if it's your pet, get on the ground with them. Making a connection with your subject means your shot will be more direct and have greater impact.

★ Check the area around your subject before you snap your perfect pic, or you might get unexpected results, like trees sprouting from heads!

★ Fed up with the usual cheesy grins and posed pics? Then make like the paparazzi and catch your friends unawares for natural, relaxed shots. Catch them reading, chatting or enjoying their fave hobby – but know when to stop. Nobody likes pictures of themselves snoring or stuffing their faces...

★ Cameras are fab for capturing memorable moments at parties...but if it's your party, you may be too busy enjoying yourself to take photos. Ask your friends to snap all the little details you may have missed, from decorations to clearing up...the results can be surprisingly funny!

★ Remember, you're in charge of the camera. Pose your subjects, add props, and experiment. Snap pictures from above and below, and at crazy angles. Take control over the way you want your pictures to look. After all, you're the artist!

So what are you waiting for? Grab your friends and have some School Friends fun!

Jess x

Now turn the page
for a sneak preview of the next
unmissable **School Friends** story...

Star
of
Silver
Spires

Chapter One

"No, I can't!" I insisted, shaking my head firmly. "Not in a million years!" I added, in case any of my friends hadn't quite got the message.

"But you're so talented, Mia!" said Georgie, my very best friend. "You play the piano like…brilliantly, and you sing like…brilliantly!"

I couldn't help laughing. She looked so funny, throwing her hands in the air dramatically, as only Georgie can.

"And that song you made up is lovely," added Naomi, smiling.

"No, I *really* can't," I repeated. "I'd just be too

scared. I mean *far* too scared!" I folded my arms, and probably looked stubborn and immature. But I couldn't help it. The thought of entering the Silver Spires junior singer/songwriter contest simply filled me with dread.

"I know what you mean about being nervous," said Grace. "I still get nervous every time I do any competitive sport."

I smiled gratefully at Grace. "And this is in front of the whole school," I said quietly. But in my heart I knew that even if it was in front of just the Year Sevens, I'd still never be able to manage it. "I'd...die."

"Which wouldn't be very helpful if you were just about to sing!" said Georgie, looking at me as though I was hopeless.

"Don't pressure her," said Naomi. "Not everyone's as outgoing as you, Georgie!"

I thanked Naomi for that, with my eyes. She's the wise one of the group and I was really pleased that she understood how I felt.

"Well I think Mia needs to be pushed!" said Jess, folding her arms. "She's just too modest!"

The five of us were sitting under one of the trees on the grass behind the main Silver Spires building. Well actually only four of us were sitting under the tree. Georgie was stretched out in the sun. She'd rolled her school skirt over at the waist to make it as short as possible, and she'd tied a knot in her shirt so her stomach could get tanned as well as her legs. It was morning break, and there were loads of other Silver Spires students dotted all over the huge grassy area, some of them lying back sunbathing, others just sitting and chatting. It was the second half of the summer term and also the beginning of the lovely hot weather. It gives me such a nice feeling to be able to look round and know that I'm a part of this beautiful place. Silver Spires is just the best boarding school in the world.

My eyes flicked round my friends and landed on Georgie. "You're getting very pink," I told her. "Did you put suncream on?"

She sighed. "Why did I have to be born with such pale skin? Why can't I be black, like Naomi? Or at least a bit darker than I am, like Grace."

Grace is from Thailand and it's true she's got lovely olive-coloured skin. She sighed and mumbled something about thinking her looks were boring, while Naomi laughed, then turned suddenly serious and stared into the distance. "We should just be happy with what we are, shouldn't we?"

I guessed she was thinking about some of the poor

people she's met in Ghana, which is the country she comes from. Naomi is actually a Ghanaian princess, but she hates people knowing that. She feels very lucky to have been born into a wealthy family, and she spends loads of time in the school holidays working for a charity that builds wells in Ghana.

"Well, I'm just as pale as you, Georgie," I quickly said, because Naomi looked sad, and I wanted to bring her back to the here and now.

"And I've got freckles but *I* don't care!" laughed Jess.

"Yes, that's another complaint I've got," Georgie said, sitting up suddenly. "I'd be fine with being pale as long as I had a 'don't care' attitude like you two!"

So then we all laughed, and I felt happy that we'd got away from the subject of the Silver Spires Star contest, because the very thought of singing my own song in front of an audience made me feel quite panicky, and I didn't like my friends trying to push me into it. It was embarrassing and pathetic that I had such a fear of performing in public, especially because music is so important to me and I love playing the piano. But what happened when I was six years old has left a terrible mark on me.

It was my first local music festival and I was playing a piece by Handel. We were all supposed to announce our pieces and say the name of the composer before we played. I remember looking out at all the faces and trying to find Mum and Dad and my baby brother, but Mum's seat was empty. It turned out that she'd had to take my little brother out because he'd started to cry, but I didn't know that at the time and I just felt frightened to see all the faces but no Mum. When I came to announce my piece, in my worried state I couldn't remember the name of the composer, but I knew it reminded me of a doorknob, so that's what I said... "'*Intermezzo*', by Door Knob." And I remember wanting to cry because I didn't understand why people started laughing. And I got so upset then that my fingers didn't seem to work properly and I played the piece terribly and got the worst mark of anyone.

The next year, my teacher tried to persuade me to enter the music festival again but I refused. When I was eight I finally agreed to give it another try, but I felt so sick when I got onto the stage that I had to run off and straight out of the hall, otherwise I would have been sick in front of the whole audience.

After that I never entered one of the town music festivals again, and neither did I play piano in concerts at my primary school, even though my teachers and then my friends tried and tried to persuade me. In the end the teachers gave up because I think Mum must have had a word with them, but my friends wouldn't leave me alone. None of them knew what had happened at the music festivals, and it was far too embarrassing to explain, so I just kept on making excuses that I'd hurt my finger or didn't have a piece ready, or even that I'd lost my music, which all seems ridiculous now.

It was a relief when the Year Six concert at my old school came and went without me having to play in it, but then I came here to Silver Spires and now it looks as though my problems are starting all over again. The real trouble is that I *should* be able to play in public, and I so wish I could. After all, *real* musicians perform in front of audiences and that's what I want to be, more than anything. Music is such a big part of my life that I ought to just make myself get over my fear…only I can't. And even if I managed, by some miracle, to play the piano in public, there are two extra layers of nervousness with this Silver Spires Star competition. You have to write the song yourself, *and* sing it.

I've only written the one song that my friends had heard in my life, and I don't know if it's any good. I wrote it almost exactly a year ago, last May, when I was in Year Six at my primary school. I was feeling really sad at the time because I knew I was going to be coming here to Silver Spires Boarding School in September, and although I was excited in some ways, I also knew I'd really miss Mum and Dad and my little brother. And I was right, because I did get homesick during the first few weeks, and I even found it hard coming back to school after the holidays for this third term. But I'm lucky because I've got the best, best friend in the world.

Georgie and I met on the induction day and then had a brilliant surprise on our first day at Silver Spires when we found we'd been put in the same dorm. The dorm is called Amethyst and it's in Hazeldean boarding house, which we naturally think is the best boarding house. There are six of us in the dorm – me, Georgie, Naomi, Katy, Grace and Jess, and we spend loads of time together. Like right now, because Katy was rushing over to us, looking very excited.

"Hiya!"

"Where've you been?" Naomi asked her.

"Bumped into Mam'zelle Clemence and guess what... She told me the Silver Spires Star contest is going to take place in the theatre! And guess what else... She's actually asked me to be part of a little committee to help decorate the theatre so it looks really striking and wow-ish! I tell you, Mia, I'm so glad I've got to know Mam'zelle Clemence through fashion club, because she's totally full of good ideas. This Star contest is going to be the coolest thing ever!"

My heart started beating too fast again. It looked like we were right back to my latest least-favourite subject.

Georgie leaned back on one elbow and squinted into the sun to look at Katy. "I'm afraid we've got a problem with our own particular star," she said, flapping a hand in my direction. "Mia doesn't want to enter."

"Oh no!" said Katy, sounding genuinely disappointed. She turned to me with pleading eyes. "I was so looking forward to sorting out your outfit."

I drew my knees up and hugged them tightly, feeling tenser than ever. I really wanted my friends to stop trying to persuade me to enter now, but I couldn't bring myself to talk about how much I hated performing in front of an audience and how it had built up over the years into this massive fear. So instead I decided it would be best to pretend it was all to do with the songwriting.

"This is turning into a nightmare!" I said, trying

to sound a bit jokey and not show how upset I really was. "Apart from that one song you've heard, Georgie – which is far too babyish anyway – I've never written any lyrics, only music." I hesitated over the next bit, but decided to say it in the end. "And anyway, I'm just not the…performing type."

Georgie suddenly sat straight up again and put her hands up like a policeman stopping the traffic. "Hold it right there! I've had a magnabulous idea!"

We all laughed. Even me – though something told me I wasn't going to like this magnabulous idea.

"*You* might not be a performer, Mamma Mia, but *yours truly* most definitely *is*! So how about *you* write the music and play the piano, and I'll write the lyrics and be the singer!" She jumped up and came to sit close beside me and gave me a hug that was a bit awkward, because I was still clasping my arms tightly round my knees, trying to protect myself from all Georgie's wild enthusiasm. I felt like if I allowed myself to relax even for a second, I might be letting myself in for the dreaded contest. "I mean that wouldn't be breaking the rules, would it?" Georgie went on. "Miss York clearly said that you can have duets or even whole bands, as long as someone in the group has actually written the song, didn't she?"

I could feel that the others were all looking at me,

waiting to hear what I'd say to this latest idea. And the truth was that I just didn't know what to say.

But deep inside my mind there was the smallest chink of maybe-that-would-be-all-right – maybe I *could* perform – beginning to show. I'd always dreamed of being a proper musician playing in front of a proper audience, and this could be my chance to prove myself if I just had the courage.

To find out what happens next, read

Star of Silver Spires

About the Author

Ann Bryant's School Days

Who was your favourite teacher?

At primary it was Mr. Perks – we called him Perksy. I was in his class in Year Six, and most days he let me work on a play I was writing! At secondary, my fave teacher was Mrs. Rowe, simply because I loved her subject (French) and she was so young and pretty and slim and chic and it was great seeing what new clothes she'd be wearing.

What were your best and worst lessons?

My brain doesn't process history, geography or science and I hated cookery, so those were my least favourite subjects. But I was good at English, music, French and PE, so I loved those. I also enjoyed art, although I was completely rubbish at it!

What was your school uniform like?

We had to wear a white shirt with a navy blue tie and sweater, and a navy skirt, but there was actually a wide variety of styles allowed – I was a very small person and liked pencil-thin skirts. We all rolled them over and over at the waist!

Did you take part in after-school activities?

Well I loved just hanging out with my friends, but most of all I loved ballet and went to extra classes in Manchester after school.

Did you have any pets while you were at school?

My parents weren't animal lovers so we were only allowed a goldfish! But since I had my two daughters, we've had loads – two cats, two guinea pigs, two rabbits, two hamsters and two goldfish.

What was your most embarrassing moment?

When I was in Year Seven I had to play piano for assembly. It was April Fool's Day and the piano wouldn't work (it turned out that someone had put a book in the back). I couldn't bring myself to stand up and investigate because that would draw attention to me, so I sat there with my hands on the keys wishing to die, until the Deputy Head came and rescued me!

To find out more about Ann Bryant visit her website: www.annbryant.co.uk

Want to know more about the
Silver Spires girls?

Or try a quiz to discover which
School Friend you're most like?

You can even send Silver Spires e-cards
to your best friends and post your own
book reviews online!

It's all at

www.silverspiresschool.co.uk

Check it out now!